A Mountain Europa

John Fox Jr.

Contents

A MOUNTAIN EUROPA

BY

John Fox Jr.

TO JAMES LANE ALLEN

I

AS Clayton rose to his feet in the still air, the tree-tops began to tremble in the gap below him, and a rippling ran through the leaves up the mountain-side. Drawing off his hat he stretched out his arms to meet it, and his eyes closed as the cool wind struck his throat and face and lifted the hair from his forehead. About him the mountains lay like a tumultuous sea-the Jellico Spur, stilled gradually on every side into vague, purple shapes against the broken rim of the sky, and Pine Mountain and the Cumberland Range racing in like breakers from the north. Under him lay Jellico Valley, and just visible in a wooded cove, whence Indian Creek crept into sight, was a mining-camp-a cluster of white cabins-from which he had climbed that afternoon. At that distance the wagon-road narrowed to a bridle-path, and the figure moving slowly along it and entering the forest at the base of the mountain was shrunk to a toy. For a moment Clayton stood with his face to the west, drinking in the air; then tightening his belt, he caught the pliant body of a sapling and swung loose from the rock. As the tree flew back, his dog sprang after him. The descent was sharp. At times he was forced to cling to the birch-tops till they lay flat on the mountain-side.

Breathless, he reached at last a bowlder from which the path was easy to the valley below, and he leaned quivering against the soft rug of moss and lichens that covered it. The shadows had crept from the foot of the mountains, darkening the valley, and lifting up the mountain-side beneath him a long, wavering line in which met the cool, deep green of the shade and the shining bronze where the sunlight still lay. Lazily following this line, his eye caught two moving shadows that darted jagged shapes into the sunlight and as quickly withdrew them. As the road wound up toward him, two figures were soon visible through the undergrowth. Presently a head bonneted in blue rose above the bushes, and Clayton's half-shut eyes opened wide and were fixed with a look of amused expectancy where a turn of the path must bring rider and beast into plain sight. Apparently some mountain girl, wearied by the climb or in a spirit of fun, had mounted her cow while driving it home; and with a smile at the thought of the confusion he would cause her, Clayton stepped around the bowlder and waited. With the slow, easy swing of climbing cattle, the beast brought its rider into view. A bag of meal lay across its shoulders, and behind this the girl-for she was plainly young-sat sidewise, with her bare feet dangling against its flank. Her face was turned toward the valley below, and her loosened bonnet half disclosed a head of bright yellow hair.

Catching sight of Clayton, the beast stopped and lifted its head, not the meek, patient face he expected to see, but a head that was wrinkled and vicious-the head of a bull. Only the sudden remembrance of a dead mountain custom saved him from utter amazement. He had heard that when beasts of burden were scarce, cows, and especially bulls, were worked in ploughs and ridden by the mountaineers, even by the women. But this had become a tradition, the humor of which greater prosperity and contact with a new civilization had taught even the mountain people to appreciate. The necessities of this girl were evidently as great as her fear of ridicule seemed small. When the brute stopped, she began striking him in the flank with her bare heel, without looking around, and as he paid no attention to such painless goading, she turned with sudden impatience and lifted a switch above his shoulders. The stick was arrested in mid-air when she saw Clayton, and then dropped harmlessly. The quick fire in her eyes died suddenly away, and for a moment the two looked at each other with mutual curiosity, but only for a moment. There was something in Clayton's gaze that displeased her. Her face clouded, and she dropped her eyes.

"G'long," she said, in a low tone. But the bull had lowered his head, and was standing with feet planted apart and tail waving uneasily. The girl looked up in alarm.

"Watch out thar! " she called out, sharply. "Call that dog off- quick!"

Clayton turned, but his dog sprang past him and began to bark. The bull, a lean, active, vicious-looking brute, answered with a snort.

"Call him off, I tell ye! " cried the girl, angrily, springing to the ground. "Git out o' the way. Don't you see he's a-comm' at ye?"

The dog leaped nimbly into the bushes, and the maddened bull was carried on by his own Impetus toward Clayton, who, with a quick spring, landed in safety in a gully below the road. When he picked himself up from the uneven ground where he had fallen, the beast had disappeared around the bowlder. The bag had fallen, and had broken open, and some of the meal was spilled on the ground. The girl, flushed and angry, stood above it.

"Look thar, now," she said. "See whut you've done. Why'n't ye call that dog off?"

"I couldn't," said Clayton, politely. " He wouldn't come. I'm sorry, very sorry."

"Can't ye manage yer own dog?" she asked, half contemptuously.

"Not always."

"Then ye oughter leave him to home, and not let him go round a-skeerin' folks' beastes." With a little gesture of indignation she stooped and began scooping up the meal in her hand.

"Let me help you," said Clayton. The girl looked up in surprise.

You go 'way," she said.

But Clayton stayed, watching her helplessly. He wanted to carry the bag for her, but she swung it to her shoulder, and moved away. He followed her around the bowlder, where his late enemy was browsing peacefully on sassafras-bushes.

"You stay thar now," said the girl, " and keep that dog back."

"Won't you let me help you get up?" he asked.

Without answering, the girl sprang lightly to the bull's back, Once only she looked around at him. He took off his hat, and a puzzled expression came into her face. Then, without a word or a nod, she rode away. Clayton watched the odd pair till the bushes hid them.

"Europa, by Jove!" he exclaimed, and he sat down in bewilderment.

She was so very odd a creature, so different from the timid mountain women who shrank with averted faces almost into the bushes when he met them. She had looked him straight in the face with steady eyes, and had spoken as though her sway over mountain and road were undisputed and he had been a wretched trespasser. She paid no attention to his apologies, and she scorned his offers of assistance. She seemed no more angered by the loss of the meal than by his incapacity to manage his dog, which seemed to typify to her his general worthlessness. He had been bruised by his fall, and she did not even ask if he were hurt. Indeed, she seemed not to care, and she had ridden away from him as though he were worth no more consideration than the stone under him.

He was amused, and a trifle irritated. How could there be such a curious growth in the mountains? he questioned, as he rose and continued the descent. There was an unusual grace about her, in spite of her masculine air. Her features were regular, the nose straight and delicate, the mouth resolute, the brow broad, and the eyes intensely blue, perhaps tender, when not flashing with anger, and altogether without the listless expression he had marked in other mountain women, and which, he had noticed, deadened into pathetic hopelessness later in life. Her figure was erect, and her manner, despite its roughness, savored of something high-born. Where could she have got that bearing? She belonged to a race whose descent, he had heard, was unmixed English; upon whose lips lingered words and forms of speech that Shakespeare had heard and used. Who could tell what blood ran in her veins?

Musing, he had come almost unconsciously to a spur of the mountains under which lay the little mining-camp. It was six o'clock, and the miners, grim and black, each with a pail in hand and a little oil-lamp in his cap, were going down from work. A shower had passed over the mountains above him, and the last sunlight, coming through a gap in the west, struck the rising mist and turned it to gold. On a rock which thrust from the mountain its gray, sombre face, half embraced by a white arm of the mist, Clayton saw the figure of a woman. He waved his hat, but the figure stood motionless, and he turned into the woods toward the camp.

It was the girl; and when Clayton disappeared she too turned and went on her way. She had stopped there because she knew he must pass a point where she might see him again. She was little less indifferent than she seemed; her motive was little more than curiosity. She had never seen that manner of man before. Evidently he was a " furriner "from the " settlemints." No man in the mountains had a smooth, round face like his, or wore such a queer hat, such a soft, white shirt, and no galluses," or carried such a shiny, weak-looking stick, or owned a dog that he couldn't make mind him. She was not wholly contemptuous, however. She had felt vaguely the meaning of his politeness and deference. She was puzzled and pleased, she scarcely knew why.

"He was mighty accomodatin'," she thought. But whut," she asked herself as she rode slowly homeward-" whut did he take off his hat fer

II

IGHTS twinkled from every cabin as Clayton passed through the camp. Outside the kitchen doors, miners, bare to the waist, were bathing their blackened faces and bodies, with children, tattered and unclean, but healthful, playing about them; within, women in loose gowns, with sleeves unrolled and with disordered hair, moved like phantoms through clouds of savory smoke. The commissary was brilliantly lighted. At a window close by improvident miners were drawing the wages of the day, while their wives waited in the store with baskets unfilled. In front of the commissary a crowd of negroes were talking, laughing, singing, and playing pranks like children. Here two, with grinning faces, were squared off, not to spar, but to knock at each other's tattered hat; there two more, with legs and arms indistinguishable, were wrestling; close by was the sound of a mouth-harp, a circle of interested spectators, and, within, two dancers pitted against each other, and shuffling with a zest that labor seemed never to affect.

Immediately after supper Clayton went to his room, lighted his lamp, and sat down to a map he was tracing. His room was next the ground, and a path ran near the open window. As he worked, every passer-by would look curiously within. On the wall above his head a pair of fencing-foils were crossed under masks. Below these hung two pistols, such as courteous Claude Duval used for side-arms. Opposite were two old rifles, and beneath them two stone beer-mugs, and a German student's pipe absurdly long and richly ornamented. A mantel close by was filled with curiosities, and near it hung a banjo unstrung, a tennis-racket, and a blazer of startling colors. Plainly they were relics of German student life, and the odd contrast they made with the rough wall and ceiling suggested a sharp change in the fortunes of the young worker beneath. Scarcely six months since he had been suddenly summoned home from Germany. The reason was vague, but having read of recent American failures, notably in Wall Street, he knew what had happened. Reaching New York, he was startled by the fear that his mother was dead, so gloomy was the house, so subdued his sister's greeting, and so worn and sad his father's face. The trouble, however, was what he had guessed, and he had accepted it with quiet resignation. The financial wreck seemed complete; but one resource, however, was left. Just after the war Clayton's father had purchased mineral lands in the South, and it was with the idea of developing these that he had encouraged the marked scientific tastes of his son, and had sent him to a German university. In view of his own disaster, and the fact that a financial tide was swelling southward, his forethought seemed an inspiration. To this resource Clayton turned eagerly; and after a few weeks at home, which were made intolerable by straitened circumstances, and the fancied coldness of friend and acquaintance, he was hard at work in the heart of the Kentucky mountains.

The transition from the careless life of a student was swift and bitter; it was like beginning a new life with a new identity, though Clayton suffered less than he anticipated. He had become interested from the first. There was nothing in the pretty glen, when he came, but a mountaineer's cabin and a few gnarled old apple-trees, the roots of which checked the musical flow of a little stream. Then the air was filled with the tense ring of hammer and saw, the mellow echoes of axes, and the shouts of ox-drivers from the forests, indignant groans from the mountains, and a little town sprang up before his eyes, and cars of shining coal wound slowly about the mountainside.

Activity like this stirred his blood. Busy from dawn to dark, he had no time to grow miserable. His work was hard, to be sure, but it made rest and sleep a luxury, and it had the new zest of independence; he even began to take in it no little pride when he found himself an essential part of the quick growth going on. When leisure came, he could take to woods filled with unknown birds, new forms of insect life, and strange plants and flowers. With every day, too, he was more deeply stirred by the changing beauty of the mountains hidden at dawn with white mists, faintly veiled through the day with an atmosphere that made him think of Italy, and enriched by sunsets of startling beauty. But strongest of all was the interest he found in the odd human mixture about him-the simple, good-natured darkies who slouched past him, magnificent in physique and picturesque with rags; occasional foreigners just from Castle Garden, with the hope of the New World still in their faces; and now and then a gaunt mountaineer stalking awkwardly in the rear of the march toward civilization. Gradually it had dawned upon him that this last, silent figure, traced through Virginia, was closely linked by blood and speech with the common people of England, and, moulded perhaps by the influences of feudalism, was still strikingly unchanged; that now it was the most distinctively national remnant on American soil, and symbolized the development of the continent, and that with it must go the last suggestions of the pioneers, with their hardy physiques, their speech, their manners and customs, their simple architecture and simple mode of life. It was soon plain to him, too, that a change was being wrought at last-the change of destruction. The older mountaineers, whose bewildered eyes watched the noisy signs of an unintelligible civilization, were passing away. Of the rest, some, sullen and restless, were selling their homesteads and following the spirit of their forefathers into a new wilderness; others, leaving their small farms in adjacent valleys to go to ruin, were gaping idly about the public works, caught up only too easily by the vicious current of the incoming tide. In a century the mountaineers must be swept away, and their ignorance of the tragic forces at work among them gave them an unconscious pathos that touched Clayton deeply.

As he grew to know them, their historical importance yielded to a genuine interest in the people themselves. They were densely ignorant, to be sure; but they were natural, simple, and hospitable. Their sense of personal worth was high, and their democracy-or aristocracy, since there was no distinction of caste-absolute. For generations, son had lived like father in an isolation hardly credible. No influence save such as shook the nation ever reached them. The Mexican war, slavery, and national politics of the first half-century were still present issues, and each old man would give his rigid, individual opinion sometimes with surprising humor and force. He went much among them, and the rugged old couples whom he found in the cabin porches-so much alike at first-quickly became distinct with a quaint individuality. Among young or old, however, he had found nothing like the half-wild young creature he had met on the mountain that day. In her a type had crossed his path-had driven him from it, in truth-that seemed unique and inexplicable. He had been little more than amused at first, but a keen interest had been growing in him with every thought of her. There was an indefinable charm about the girl. She gave a new and sudden zest to his interest in mountain life; and while he worked, the incidents of the encounter on the mountain came minutely back to him till he saw her again as she rode away, her supple figure swaying with every movement of the beast, and dappled with quivering circles of sunlight from the bushes, her face calm, but still flushed with color, and her yellow hair shaking about her shoulders-not lustreless and flaxen, as hair was in the mountains, he remembered, but catching the sunlight like gold.

Almost unconsciously he laid aside his pencil and leaned from his window to lift his eyes to the dark mountain he had climbed that day. The rude melody of an old-fashioned hymn was coming up the glen, and he recognized the thin, quavering voice of an old mountaineer, Uncle Tommy Brooks, as he was familiarly known, whose cabin stood in the midst of the camp, a pathetic contrast to the smart new houses that had sprung around it. The old man had lived in the glen for nearly three-quarters of a century, and he, if any one, must know the girl. With the thought, Clayton sprang through the window, and a few minutes later was at the cabin. The old man sat whittling in the porch, joining in the song with which his wife was crooning a child to sleep within. Clayton easily identified Europa, as he had christened her; the simple mention of her means of transport was sufficient.

Ridin' a bull, was she? " repeated the old man, laughing. "Well, that was Easter Hicks, old Bill Hicks' gal. She's a sort o' connection o' mine. Me and Bill married cousins.

She's a cur'us critter as ever I seed. She don' seem to take atter her dad nur her mammy nother, though Bill allus had a quar streak in 'im, and was the wust man I ever seed when he was disguised by licker. Whar does she live? Oh, up thar, right on top o' Wolf Mountain, with her mammy."

Alone?

"Yes; fer her dad ain't thar. No; 'n' he ain't dead. I'll tell ye"-the old man lowered his tone-" thar used to be a big lot o' moonshinin' done in these parts, 'n' a raider come hyeh to see 'bout it. Well, one mornin' he was found layin' in the road with a bullet through him. Bill was s'picioned. Now, I ain't a-sayin' as Bill done it, but when a whole lot more rode up thar on hosses one night, they didn't find Bill. They hain't found him yit, fer he's out in the mountains somewhar a-hidin'."

"How do they get along without him?" asked Clayton.

"Why, the gal does the work. She ploughs with that bull, and does the plantin' herself. She kin chop wood like a man. An' as fer shootin', well, when huntin's good 'n' thar's shootin'-matches round-about, she don't have to buy much meat."

"It's a wonder some young fellow hasn't married her. I suppose, though, she's too young."

The old man laughed. "Thar's been many a lively young fellow that's tried it, but she's hard to ketch as a wildcat. She won't have nothin' to do with other folks, 'n' she nuver comes down hyeh into the valley, 'cept to git her corn groun' er to shoot a turkey. Sherd Raines goes up to see her, and folks say he air tryin' to git her into the church. But the gal won't go nigh a meetin'-house. She air a cur'us critter," he concluded emphatically, " shy as a deer till she air stirred up, and then she air a caution; mighty gentle sometimes, and ag'in stubborn as a mule."

A shrill, infantile scream came from within, and the old man paused a moment to listen.

"Ye didn't know I had a great-grandchild, did ye? That's it a-hollerin'. Talk about Easter bein' too young to merry! Why hit's mother air two year younger'n Easter. Jes come in hyeh a minit." The old mountaineer rose and led the way into the cabin. Clayton was embarrassed at first. On one bed lay a rather comely young woman with a child by her side; on a chest close by sat another with her lover, courting in the most open and primitive manner. In the corner an old grandam dozed with her pipe, her withered face just touched by the rim of the firelight. Near a rectangular hole in the wall which served the purpose of a window, stood a girl whose face, silhouetted against the darkness, had in it a curious mixture of childishness and maturity.

"Whar's the baby? " asked Uncle Tommy.

Somebody outside was admiring it, and the young girl leaned through the window and lifted the infant within.

Thar's a baby fer ye! " exclaimed the old mountaineer, proudly, lifting it in the air and turning its face to the light. But the child was peevish and fretful, and he handed it back gently. Clayton was wondering which was the mother, when, to his amazement, almost to his confusion, the girl lifted the child calmly to her own breast. The child was the mother of the child. She was barely fifteen, with the face of a girl of twelve, and her motherly manner had struck him as an odd contrast. He felt a thrill of pity for the young mother as he called to mind the aged young wives he had seen who were haggard and care-worn at thirty, and who still managed to live to an old age. He was indefinably glad that Easter had escaped such a fate. When he left the cabin, the old man called after him from the door:

"Thar's goin' to be a shootin'-match among the boys to-morrer, 'n' I jedge that Easter '11 be on hand. She al'ays is."

"Is that so? " said Clayton. " Well, I'll look out for it."

The old mountaineer lowered his voice.

"Ye hain't thinkin' about takin' a wife, air ye?"

"No, no!"

" Well, ef ye air," said the old man, slowly, "I'm a-thinkin' yu'll have to buck up ag'in Sherd Raines, fer ef I hain't like a goose a-pickin' o' grass by moonshine, Sherd air atter the gal fer hisself, not fer the Lord. Yes," he continued, after a short, dry laugh; "'n' mebbe ye'll hav to keep an eye open fer old Bill. They say that he air mighty low down, 'n' kind o' sorry 'n' skeery, for I reckon Sherd Raines hev told him he hav got to pay the penalty fer takin' a human life; but I wouldn't sot much on his bein' sorry ef he was mad at me and had licker in him. He hates furriners, and he has a crazy idee that they is all raiders 'n' lookin' fer him."

"I don't think I'll bother him," said Clayton, turning away with a laugh. "Good-night t" With a little cackle of incredulity, the old man closed the door. The camp had sunk now to perfect quiet; but for the faint notes of a banjo far up the glen, not a sound trembled on the night air.

The rim of the moon was just visible above the mountain on which Easter-what a pretty name that was !-had flashed upon his vision with such theatric effect. As its brilliant light came slowly down the dark mountain-side, the mists seemed to loosen their white arms, and to creep away like ghosts mistaking the light for dawn. With the base of the mountain in dense shadow, its crest, uplifted through the vapors, seemed poised in the air at a startling height. Yet it was near the crest that he had met her. Clayton paused a moment, when he reached his door, to look again. Where in that cloud-land could she live?

III

WHEN the great bell struck the hour of the next noon, mountaineers with long rifles across their shoulders were moving through the camp. The glen opened into a valley, which, blocked on the east by Pine Mountain, was thus shut in on every side by wooded heights. Here the marksmen gathered. All were mountaineers, lank, bearded, men, coatless for the most part, and dressed in brown home-made jeans, slouched, formless hats, and high, coarse boots. Sun and wind had tanned their faces to sympathy, in color, with their clothes, which had the dun look of the soil. They seemed peculiarly a race of the soil, to have sprung as they were from the earth, which had left indelible stains upon them. All carried long rifles, old-fashioned and home-made, some even with flint-locks. It was Saturday, and many of their wives had come with them to the camp. These stood near, huddled into a listless group, with their faces half hidden in check bonnets of various colors. A barbaric love of color was apparent in bonnet, shawl, and gown, and surprisingly in contrast with such crudeness of taste was a face when fully seen, so modest was it. The features were always delicately wrought, and softened sometimes by a look of patient suffering almost into refinement.

On the other side of the contestants were the people of the camp, a few miners with pipes lounging on the ground, and women and girls, who returned the furtive glances of the mountain women with stares of curiosity and low laughter.

Clayton had been delayed by his work, and the match was already going on when he reached the grounds.

"You've missed mighty fine shootin'," said Uncle Tommy Brooks, who was squatted on the ground near the group of marksmen.

Sherd's been a-beatin' ever'body. I'm afeard Easter hain't a-comm'. The match is 'most over now. Ef she'd been here, I don't think Sherd would 'a' got the ch'ice parts o' that beef so easy."

"Which is he? " asked Clayton.

That tall feller thar loadin' his gun."

"What did you say his name was?

" Sherd Raines, the feller that's goin' to be our circuit-rider."

He remembered the peculiar name. So this was Easter's lover. Clayton looked at the young mountaineer, curiously at first, and then with growing interest. His quiet air of authority among his fellows was like a birthright; it seemed assumed and accepted unconsciously. His face was smooth, and he was fuller in figure than the rest, but still sinewy and lank, though not awkward; his movements were too quick and decisive for that. With a casual glance Clayton had wondered what secret influence could have turned to spiritual things a man so merely animal-like in face and physique; but when the mountaineer thrust back his hat, elemental strength and seriousness were apparent in the square brow, the steady eye, the poise of the head, and in lines around the strong mouth and chin in which the struggle for self-mastery had been traced.

As the mountaineer thrust his ramrod back into its casing, he glanced at the woods behind Clayton, and said something to his companions. They, too, raised their eyes, and at the same moment the old mountaineer plucked Clayton by the sleeve.

"Thar comes Easter now."

The girl had just emerged from the edge of the forest, and with a rifle on one shoulder and a bullet-pouch and powder-horn swung from the other, was slowly coming down the path.

" Why, how air ye, Easter? " cried the old man, heartily. " Goin' to shoot, air ye? I 'lowed ye wouldn't miss this. Ye air mighty late, though."

Oh, I only wanted a turkey," said the girl. "Well, I'm a-comm' up to eat dinner with ye to-morrer," he answered, with a laugh, " fer I know ye'll git one. Y'u're on hand fer most o' the matches now. Wild turkeys must be a-gittin' skeerce."

The girl smiled, showing a row of brilliant teeth between her thin, red lips, and, without answering, moved toward the group of mountain women. Clayton had raised his hand to his hat when the old man addressed her, but he dropped it quickly to his side in no little embarrassment when the girl carelessly glanced over him with no sign of recognition. Her rifle was an old flint-lock of light build, but nearly six feet in length, with a shade of rusty tin two feet long fastened to the barrel to prevent the sunlight from affecting the marksman's aim. She wore a man's hat, which, with unintentional coquetry, was perched on one side of her head. Her hair was short, and fell as it pleased about her neck. She was bare-footed, and apparently clad in a single garment, a blue homespun gown, gathered loosely at her uncorseted waist, and showing the outline of the bust and every movement of the tall, supple form beneath. Her appearance had quickened the interest of the spectators, and apparently was a disturbing influence among the contestants, who were gathered together, evidently in dispute. From their glances Clayton saw that Easter was the subject of it.

"I guess they don't want her to shoot-them that hain't won nothin'," said Uncle Tommy.

She hev come in late," Clayton heard one say, " 'n' she oughtn' to shoot. Thar hain't no chance shootin' ag'in her noways, 'n' I'm in favor o' barrin' her out."

Oh no; let her shoot "-the voice was Raines's. "Thar hain't nothin' but a few turkeys left, 'n' ye'd better bar out the gun 'stid o' the gal, anyway, fer that gun kin outshoot any-thing in the mountains."

The girl had been silently watching the group as if puzzled; and when Raines spoke her face tightened with sudden decision, and she strode swiftly toward them in time to overhear the young mountaineer's last words.

So hit's the gun, is hit, Sherd Raines?

The crowd turned, and Raines shrank a little as the girl faced him with flashing eyes. "So hit's the gun, is hit? Hit is a good gun, but ye ought to be ashamed to take all the credit 'way from me. But ef you air so sartain hit's the gun," she continued, "I'll shoot yourn, 'n' y'u kin hev mine ef I don't beat ye with yer own gun."

"Good fer you, Easter!" shouted the old mountaineer.

Raines had recovered himself, and was looking at the girl seriously. Several of his companions urged him aloud to accept the challenge, but he paid no heed to them. He seemed to be debating the question with himself, and a moment later he said, quietly:

"'N' you kin hev mine ef I don't beat you."

This was all he said, but he kept his eyes fixed on the girl's face; and when, with a defiant glance, she turned toward the mountain women, he followed and stopped her.

"Easter," Clayton heard him say, in a low, slow voice, "I was tryin' to git ye a chance to shoot, fer ye hev been winnin' so much that it's hard to git up a match when ye air in it." The hard look on the girl's face remained unchanged, and the mountaineer continued, firmly:

"'N' I told the truth; fer ef ye pin me down, I do think hit is the gun."

" Jes you wait 'n' see," answered the girl, shortly, and Raines, after a questioning look, rejoined the group.

"I won't take the gun ef I win it," he said to them; "but she air gittin' too set up an' proud, 'n' I'm goin' to do my best to take her down a bit."

There was nothing boastful or malicious in his manner or speech, and nobody doubted that he would win, for there were few marksmen in the mountains his equals, and he would have the advantage of using his own gun.

"Look hyeh," said a long, thin mountaineer, coming up to the group, "thar ain't but one turkey left, 'n' I'd like to know what we air goin' to shoot at ef Sherd 'n' Easter gits a crack at him."

In the interest of the match no one had thought of that, and a moment of debate followed, which Clayton ended by stepping forward.

"I'll furnish a turkey for the rest of you," he said.

The girl turned when he spoke and gave him a quick glance, but averted her eyes instantly.

Clayton's offer was accepted, and the preliminary trial to decide who should shoot first at the turkey was begun. Every detail was watched with increasing interest. A piece of white paper marked with two concentric circles was placed sixty yards away, and Raines won with a bullet in the inner circle. The girl had missed both, and the mountaineer offered her two more shots to accustom herself to the gun. She accepted, and smiled a little triumphantly as she touched the outer circle with one bullet and placed the other almost in the centre. It was plain that the two were evenly matched, and several shouts of approval came from the crowd. The turkey was hobbled to a stake at the same distance, and both were to fire at its head, with the privilege of shooting at fifty yards if no rest were taken.

Raines shot first without rest, and, as he missed, the girl followed his example. The turkey dozed on in the sunlight, undisturbed by either. The mountaineer was vexed. With his powerful face set determinedly, he lay down flat on the ground, and, resting his rifle over a small log, took an inordinately long and careful aim. The rifle cracked, the turkey bobbed its head unhurt, and the marksman sprang to his feet with an exclamation of surprise and chagrin. As he loaded the gun and gravely handed it to the girl, the excitement grew intense. The crowd pressed close. The stolid faces of the mountaineer women, thrust from their bonnets, became almost eager with interest. Raines, quiet and composed as he was, looked anxious. All eyes followed every movement of the girl as she coolly stretched her long, active figure on the ground, drew her dress close about it, and, throwing her yellow hair over her face to shade her eyes from the slanting sunlight, placed her cheek against the stock of the gun. A long suspense followed. A hush almost of solemnity fell upon the crowd.

"Why don't the gal shoot?" asked a voice, impatiently.

Clayton saw what the matter was, and, stepping toward her, said quietly, "You forgot to set the trigger."

The girl's face colored. Again her eye glanced along the barrel, a puff of smoke flew from the gun, and a shout came from every pair of lips as the turkey leaped into the air and fell, beating the ground with its wings. In an instant a young mountaineer had rushed forward and seized it, and, after a glance, dropped it with a yell of triumph.

"Shot plum' through the eyes!" he shouted. "Shot plum' through the eyes!

The girl arose, and handed the gun back to Raines.

Keep hit," he said, steadily. " Hit's yourn."

"I don't want the gun," she said, "but I did want that turkey-' n' "-a little tauntingly-"I did want to beat you, Sherd Raines."

The mountaineer's face flushed and darkened, but he said nothing. He took no part in the shooting that followed, and when, after the match was over, the girl, with her rifle on one shoulder and the turkey over the other, turned up the mountain path, Clayton saw him follow her.

IV

A FORTNIGHT later Clayton, rifle in hand, took the same path. It was late in May. The 'leafage was luxuriant, and the mountains, wooded to the tops, seemed overspread with great, shaggy rugs of green. The woods were resonant with song-birds, and the dew dripped and sparkled wherever a shaft of sunlight pierced the thick leaves. Late violets hid shyly under canopies of May-apple; bunches of blue and of white anemone nodded from under fallen trees, and water ran like hidden music everywhere. Slowly the valley and the sound of its life-the lowing of cattle, the clatter at the mines, the songs of the negroes at work-sank beneath him. The chorus of birds dwindled until only the cool, flute-like notes of a wood- thrush rose faintly from below. Up he went, winding around great oaks, fallen trunks, loose bowlders, and threatening cliffs until light glimmered whitely between the boles of the trees. From a gap where he paused to rest, a fire-scald " was visible close to the' crest of the adjoining mountain. It was filled with the charred, ghost-like trunks of trees that had been burned standing. Easter's home must be near that, Clayton thought, and he turned toward it by a path that ran along the top of the mountain. After a few hundred yards the path swerved sharply through a dense thicket, and Clayton stopped in wonder.

Some natural agent had hollowed the mountain, leaving a level plateau of several acres. The earth had fallen away from a great sombre cliff of solid rock, and clinging like a swallow's nest in a cleft of this was the usual rude cabin of a mountaineer. The face of the rock was dark with vines, and the cabin was protected as by a fortress. But one way of approach was possible, and that straight to the porch. From the cliff the vines had crept to roof and chimney, and were waving their tendrils about a thin blue spiral of smoke. The cabin was gray and tottering with age. Above the porch on the branches of an apple-tree hung leaves that matched in richness of tint the thick moss on the rough shingles. Under it an old woman sat spinning, and a hound lay asleep at her feet. Easter was nowhere to be seen, but her voice came from below him in a loud tone of command; and presently she appeared from behind a knoll, above which the thatched roof of a stable was visible, and slowly ascended the path to the house. She had evidently just finished work, for a plough stood in the last furrow of the field, and the fragrance of freshly turned earth was in the air. On the porch she sank wearily into a low chair, and, folding her hands, looked away to the mountains.

Clayton climbed the crumbling fence. A dead twig snapped, and, startled by the sound, the girl began to rise; but, giving him one quick, sharp look, dropped her eyes to her hands, and remained motionless.

"Good morning," said Clayton, lifting his hat. The girl did not raise her face. The wheel stopped, and the spinner turned her head.

How air ye? " she said, with ready hospitality. " Come in an' hev a cheer."

"No, thank you," he answered, a little embarrassed by Easter's odd behavior. " May I get some water?"

"Sartinly," said the old woman, looking him over curiously. " Easter, go git some fresh."

The girl started to rise, but Clayton, picking up the bucket, said, quickly:

"Oh no; I won't trouble you. I see the spring," he added, noticing a tiny stream that trickled from a fissure at the base of the cliff.

Who air that feller, Easter? " the mother asked, in a low voice, when Clayton was out of hearing.

"One o' them furriners who hev come into Injun Creek," was the indifferent reply.

That's splendid water," said Clayton, returning. "May I give you some?" The old woman shook her head. Easter's eyes were still on the mountains, and apparently she had not heard him.

"Hit air good water," said the mother. "That spring never does go dry. You better come in and rest a spell. I suppose ye air from the mines?" she added, as she turned to resume spinning.

Yes," answered Clayton. "There is good hunting around here, isn't there? " he went on, feeling that some explanation was due for his sudden arrival away up in that lone spot.

There was no answer. Easter did not look toward him, and the spinning stopped.

"Whut d'you say?" asked the old woman.

Clayton repeated his question.

"Thar used to be prime huntin' in these parts when my dad cleared off this spot more'n fifty year ago, but the varmints hev mostly been killed out. But Easter kin tell you better'n I kin, for she does all our huntin', 'n' she kin outshoot 'mos' any man in the mountains."

Yes; I saw her shoot at the match the other day down at the mines."

Did ye? "-a smile of pleasure broke over the old woman's face-" whar she beat Sherd Raines? Sherd wanted to mortify her, but she mortified him, I reckon."

The girl did not join in her mother's laugh, though the corners of her mouth twitched faintly.

I like shooting, myself," said Clayton. "I would go into a match, but I'm afraid I wouldn't have much chance."

"I reckon not, with that short thing? " said the old woman, pointing at his repeating-rifle. "Would ye shoot with that?"

Oh, yes," answered Clayton, smiling; "it shoots very well."

"How fer?"

"Oh, a long way."

A huge shadow swept over the house, thrown by a buzzard sailing with magnificent ease high above them. Thinking that he might disturb its flight, Clayton rose and cocked his rifle.

"Ye're not going to shoot at that?" said the old woman, grinning. The girl had looked toward him at last, with a smile of faint dension.

Clayton took aim quickly and fired. The huge bird sank as though hit, curved downward, and with one flap of his great wings sailed on.

"Well, ef I didn't think ye had hit him!"said the old woman, in amazement. "You kin shoot, fer a fac'."

Easter's attention was gained at last. For the first time she looked straight at him, and her little smile of derision had given way to a look of mingled curiosity and respect.

"I expected only to scare him," said Clayton.

The gun will carry twice that far."

Hit's jest as well ye didn't hit him," said the old woman. 'Hit air five dollars fine to kill a buzzard around hyeh. I'd never thought that little thing could shoot."

"It shoots several times," said Clayton. "Hit does whut?"

Like a pistol," he explained, and, rising, he directed several shots in quick succession at a dead tree in the ploughed field. At each shot a puff of dust came almost from the same spot.

When he turned, Easter had risen to her feet in astonishment, and the mother was laughing long and loudly.

"Don't ye wish ye had a gun like that, Easter? " she cried.

Clayton turned quickly to the girl, and began explaining the mechanism of the gun to her, without appearing to notice her embarrassment, for she shrank perceptibly when he spoke to her.

"Won't you let me see your gun? " he asked.

She brought out the old flint-lock, and handed it to him almost timidly.

This is very interesting," he said. " I never saw one like it before."

"Thar hain't but one more jest like that in the mountains," said the old woman, " 'n' Easter's got that. My dad made 'em both."

"How would you like to trade one for mine, if you have two?" said Clayton to the girl. "I'll give you all my cartridges to boot."

The girl looked at her mother with hesitation. Clayton saw that both wondered what he could want with the gun, and he added:

"I'd like to have it to take home with me. It would be a great curiosity."

"Well," said the mother, "you kin hev one ef ye want hit, and think the trade's fa'r."

Clayton insisted, and the trade was made. The old woman resumed spinning. The girl took her seat in the low chair, holding her new treasure in her lap, with her eyes fixed on it, and occasionally running one brown hand down its shining barrel. Clayton watched her. She had given no sign whatever that she had ever seen him before, and yet a curious change had come over her. Her imperious manner had yielded to a singular reserve and timidity. The peculiar beauty of the girl struck him now with unusual force. Her profile was remarkably regular and delicate; her mouth small, resolute, and sensitive; heavy, dark lashes shaded her downcast eyes; and her brow suggested a mentality that he felt a strong desire to test. Her feet were small, and so were her quick, nervous hands, which were still finely shaped, in spite of the hard usage that had left them brown and callous. He wondered if she was really as lovely as she seemed; if his standard might not have been affected by his long stay in the mountains; if her picturesque environment might not have influenced his judgment. He tried to imagine her daintily slippered, clad in white, with her loose hair gathered in a Psyche knot; or in evening dress, with arms and throat bare; but the pictures were difficult to make. He liked her best as she was, in perfect physical sympathy with the natural phases about her; as much a part of them as tree, plant, or flower, embodying the freedom, grace, and beauty of nature as well and as unconsciously as they. He questioned whether she hardly felt herself to be apart from them; and, of course, she as little knew her kinship to them.

She had lifted her eyes now, and had fixed them with tender thoughtfulness on the mountains. What did she see in the scene before her, he wondered: the deep valley, brilliant with early sunshine; the magnificent sweep of wooded slopes; Pine Mountain and the peak-like Narrows, where through it the river had worn its patient way; and the Cumberland Range, lying like a cloud against the horizon, and bluer and softer than the sky above it. He longed to know what her thoughts were; if in them there might be a hint of what he hoped to find. Probably she could not tell them, should he ask her, so unconscious was she of her mental life, whatever that might be. Indeed, she seemed scarcely to know of her own existence; there was about her a simplicity to which he had felt himself rise only in the presence of the spirit about some lonely mountain-top or in the heart of deep woods. Her gaze was not vacant, not listless, but the pensive look of a sensitive child, and Clayton let himself fancy that there was in it an unconscious love of the beauty before her, and of its spiritual suggestiveness a slumbering sense, perhaps easily awakened. Perhaps he might awaken it.

The drowsy hum of the spinning-wheel ceased suddenly, and his dream was shattered. He wondered how long they had sat there saying nothing, and how long the silence might continue. Easter, he believed, would never address him. Even the temporary intimacy that the barter of the gun had brought about was gone. The girl seemed lost in unconsciousness. The mother had gone to her loom, and was humming softly to herself as she passed the shuttle to and fro. Clayton turned for an instant to watch her, and the rude background, which he had forgotten, thrust every unwelcome detail upon his attention: the old cabin, built of hewn logs, held together by wooden pin and augur-hole, and shingled with rough boards; the dark, windowless room; the unplastered walls; the beds with old-fashioned high posts, mattresses of straw, and cords instead of slats; the home-made chairs with straight backs, tipped with carved knobs; the mantel filled with utensils and overhung with bunches of drying herbs; a ladder with half a dozen smooth-worn steps leading to the loft; and a wide, deep fireplace-the only suggestion of cheer and comfort in the gloomy interior. An open porch connected the single room with the kitchen. Here, too, were suggestions of daily duties. The mother's face told a tale of hardship and toil, and there was the plough in the furrow, and the girl's calloused hands folded in her lap. With a thrill of compassion Clayton turned to her. What a pity! what a pity! Just now her face had the peace of a child's; but when aroused, an electric fire burned from her calm eyes and showed the ardent temperament that really lay beneath. If she were quick and sympathetic-and she must be, he who could tell how rich the development possible for her?

"You hain't seen much of this country, I reckon. You hain't been here afore?

The mother had broken the silence at last.

No," said Clayton; "but I like it very much."

Do ye? " she asked, in surprise. " Why, I 'lowed you folks from the settlemints thought hit was mighty scraggy down hyeh."

"Oh no. These mountains and woods are beautiful, and I never saw lovelier beech-trees. The coloring of their trunks is so exquisite, and the shade is so fine," he concluded, lamely, noticing a blank look on the old woman's face. To his delight the girl, half turned toward him, was listening with puzzled interest.

Well," said the old woman, " beeches is beautiful to me when they has mast enough to feed the hogs."

Carried back to his train of speculations, Clayton started at this abrupt deliverance. There was a suspicion of humor in the old woman's tone that showed an appreciation of their different standpoints. It was lost on Clayton, however, for his attention had been caught by the word "mast," which, by some accident, he I had never heard before.

" Mast," he asked, " what is that?

The girl looked toward him in amazement, and burst into a low, suppressed laugh. Her mother explained the word, and all laughed heartily.

Clayton soon saw that his confession of ignorance was a lucky accident. It brought Easter and himself nearer common ground. She felt that there was something, after all, that she could teach him. She had been overpowered by his politeness and deference and his unusual language, and, not knowing what they meant, was overcome by a sense of her inferiority. The incident gave him the key to his future conduct. A moment later she looked up covertly, and, meeting his eyes, laughed again. The ice was broken. He began to wonder if she really had noticed him so little at their first meeting as not to recognize him, or if her indifference or reserve had prevented her from showing the recognition. He pulled out his notebook and began sketching rapidly, conscious that the girl was watching him. When be finished, he rose, picking up the old flint-lock.

"Won't ye stay and hev some dinner?,' asked the old woman.

"No, thank you."

Come ag'in," she said, cordially, adding the mountaineer's farewell, "I wish ye well."

"Thank you, I will. Good-day."

As he passed the girl he paused a moment and dropped the paper into her lap. It was a rude sketch of their first meeting, the bull coming at him like a tornado. The color came to her face, and when Clayton turned the corner of the house he heard her laughing.

"What you laughin' at, Easter?" asked the mother, stopping her work and looking around.

For answer the girl rose and walked into the house, hiding the paper in her bosom. The old woman watched her narrowly.

I never seed ye afeard of a man afore," she said to herself. "No, nur so tickled 'bout one, nother. Well, he air as accommodatin' a feller as I ever see, ef he air a furriner. But he was a fool to swop his gun fer hem."

V

THEREAFTER Clayton saw the girl whenever possible. If she came to the camp, he walked up the mountain with her. No idle day passed that he did not visit the cabin, and it was not long before he found himself strangely interested. Her beauty and fearlessness had drawn him at first; her indifference and stolidity had piqued him; and now the shyness that displaced these was inconsistent and puzzling. This he set himself deliberately at work to remove, and the conscious effort gave a peculiar piquancy to their intercourse. He had learned the secret of association with the mountaineers-to be as little unlike them as possible-and he put the knowledge into practice. He discarded coat and waistcoat, wore a slouched hat, and went unshaven for weeks. He avoided all conventionalities, and was as simple in manner and speech as possible. Often when talking with Easter, her face was blankly unresponsive, and a question would sometimes leave her in confused silence. He found it necessary to use the simplest Anglo-Saxon words, and he soon fell into many of the quaint expressions of the mountaineers and their odd, slow way of speech. This course was effective, and in time the shyness wore away and left between them a comradeship as pleasant as unique. Sometimes they took long walks together on the mountains. This was contrary to mountain etiquette, but they were remote even from the rude conventionalities of the life below them. They even went hunting together, and Easter had the joy of a child when she discovered her superiority to Clayton in woodcraft and in the use of a rifle. If he could tell her the names of plants and flowers they found, and how they were akin, she could show him where they grew. If he could teach her a little more about animals and their habits than she already knew, he had always to follow her in the search for game. Their fellowship was, in consequence, never more complete than when they were roaming the woods. In them Easter was at home, and her ardent nature came to the surface like a poetic glow from her buoyant health and beauty. Then appeared all that was wayward and elfin-like in her character, and she would be as playful, wilful, evanescent as a wood-spirit. Sometimes, when they were separated, she would lead him into a ravine by imitating a squirrel or a wild-turkey, and, as he crept noiselessly along with bated breath and eyes peering eagerly through the tree-tops or the underbrush, she would step like a dryad from behind some tree at his side, with a ringing laugh at his discomfiture. Again, she might startle him by running lightly along the fallen trunk of a tree that lay across a torrent, or, in a freak of wilfulness, would let herself down the bare face of some steep cliff. If he scolded her, she laughed. If he grew angry, she was serious instantly, and once she fell to weeping and fled home. He followed her, but she barricaded herself in her room in the loft, and would not be coaxed down. The next day she had forgotten that she was angry.

Her mother showed no surprise at any of her moods. Easter was not like other " gals," she said; she had always been" quar," and she reckoned would" al'ays be that way." She objected in no wise to Clayton's intimacy with her. The furriner," she told Raines, was the only man who had ever been able to manage her, and if she wanted Easter to do anything " ag'in her will, she went to him fust "-a simple remark that threw the mountaineer into deep thoughtfulness.

Indeed, this sense of power that Clayton felt over the wilful, passionate creature thrilled him with more pleasure than he would have been willing to admit; at the same time it suggested to him a certain responsibility. Why not make use of it, and a good use? The girl was perhaps deplorably ignorant, could do but little more than read and write; but she was susceptible of development, and at times apparently conscious of the need of it and desirous for it. Once he had carried her a handful of violets, and thereafter an old pitcher that stood on a shelf blossomed every day with wild-flowers. He had transplanted a vine from the woods and taught her to train it over the porch, and the first hint of tenderness he found in her nature was in the care of that plant. He had taken her a book full of pictures and fashion-plates, and he had noticed a quick and ingenious adoption of some of its hints in her dress.

One afternoon, as he lay on his bed in a darkened corner of his room, a woman's shadow passed across the wall, returned, and a moment later he saw Easter's face at the window. He had lain quiet, and watched her while her wondering eyes roved from one object to another, until they were fastened with a long, intent look on a picture that stood upon a table near the window. He stirred, and her face melted away instantly. A few days later he was sitting with Easter and Raines at the cabin. The mother was at the other end of the porch, talking to a neighbor who had stopped to rest on his way across the mountains.

Easter air a-gettin' high notions," she was saying, " 'n' she air a-spendin' her savin 's, 'n' all mine she kin git hold of, to buy fixin's at the commissary. She must hev white crockery, 'n' towels, 'n' newfangled forks, 'n' sichlike." A conscious flush came into the girl's face, and she rose hastily and went into the house.

"I was afeard," continued the mother, " that she would hev her hair cut short, 'n' be a-flyin' with ribbons, 'n' spangled out like a rainbow, like old 'Lige Hicks's gal, ef I hadn't heerd the furriner tell her it was ' beastly.' Thar ain't no fear now, fer what that furriner don't like, Easter don't nother."

For an instant the mountaineer's eyes had flashed on Clayton, but when the latter, a trifle embarrassed, looked up, Raines apparently had heard nothing. Easter did not reappear until the mountaineer was gone.

There were other hopeful signs. Whenever Clayton spoke of his friends, she always listened eagerly, and asked innumerable questions about them. If his attention was caught by any queer custom or phrase of the mountain dialect, she was quick to ask in return how he would say the same thing, and what the custom was in the settlemints." She even made feeble attempts to model her own speech after his.

In a conscious glow that he imagined was philanthropy, Clayton began his task of elevation. She was not so ignorant as he had supposed. Apparently she had been taught by somebody, but when asked by whom, she hesitated answering; and he had taken it for granted that what she knew she had puzzled out alone. He was astonished by her quickness, her docility, and the passionate energy with which she worked. Her instant obedience to every suggestion, her trust in every word he uttered, made him acutely and at times uncomfortably conscious of his responsibility. At the same time there was in the task something of the pleasure that a young sculptor feels when, for the first time, the clay begins to yield obedience to his fingers, and something of the delight that must have thrilled Pygmalion when he saw his statue tremulous with conscious life.

VI

THE possibility of lifting the girl above her own people, and of creating a spirit of discontent that might embitter her whole life, had occurred to Clayton; but at such moments the figure of Raines came into the philanthropic picture forming slowly in his mind, and his conscience was quieted. He could see them together; the gradual change that Easter would bring about in him, the influence of the two on their fellows. The mining-camp grew into a town with a modest church on the outskirts, and a cottage where Raines and Easter were installed. They stood between the old civilization and the new, understanding both, and protecting the native strength of the one from the vices of the other, and training it after more breadth and refinement. But Raines and Easter did not lend themselves to the picture so readily, and gradually it grew vague and shadowy, and the figure of the mountaineer was blurred.

Clayton did not bring harmony to the two. At first he saw nothing of the mountaineer, and when they met at the cabin Raines remained only a short time. If Easter cared for him at all, she did not show it. How he was regarded by the mother, Clayton had learned long ago, when, in answer to one of his questions, she had said, with a look at Easter, that " Raines was the likeliest young feller in them mountains "; that "he knew morn'n anybody round thar"; that " he had spent a year in the settlemints, was mighty religious, and would one day be a circuit-rider. Anyhow," she concluded, " he was a mighty good friend o' theirn."

But as for Easter, she treated him with unvarying indifference, though Clayton noticed she was more quiet and reserved in the mountaineer's presence; and, what was unintelligible to him, she refused to speak of her studies when Raines was at the cabin, and warned her mother with an angry frown when the latter began telling the mountaineer of "whut a change had come over Easter, and how she reckoned the gal was a-gittin' eddicated enough fer to teach anybody in the mountains, she was a-larnin' so much."

After that little incident, he met Raines at the cabin oftener. The mountaineer was always taciturn, though he listened closely when anything was said, and even when addressed by Easter's mother his attention, Clayton noticed, was fixed on Easter and himself. He felt that he was being watched, and it irritated him. He had tried to be friendly with the mountaineer, but his advances were received with a reserve that was almost suspicion. As time went on, the mountaineer's visits increased in frequency and in length, and at last one night he stayed so long that, for the first time, Clayton left him there.

Neither spoke after the young engineer was gone. The mountaineer sat looking closely at Easter, who was listlessly watching the moon as it rose above the Cumberland Range and brought into view the wavering outline of Pine Mountain and the shadowed valley below. It was evident from his face and his eyes, which glowed with the suppressed fire of some powerful emotion within, that he had remained for a purpose; and when he rose and said, "I reckon I better be a-goin', Easter," his voice was so unnatural that the girl looked up quickly.

Hit air late," she said, after a slight pause.

His face flushed, but he set his lips and caught the back of his chair, as though to steady himself.

"I reckon," he said, with slow bitterness, "that hit would 'a' been early long as the furriner was hyeh."

The girl was roused instantly, but she said nothing, and he continued, in a determined tone:

"Easter, thar's a good deal I've wanted to say to ye fer a long time, but I hev kept a-puttin' hit off until I'm afeard maybe hit air too late. But I'm a-goin' to say hit now, and I want ye to listen." He cleared his throat huskily. " Do ye know, Easter, what folks in the mountains is a-sayin'?

The girl's quick insight told her what was coming, and her face hardened.

"Have ye ever knowed me, Sherd Raines, to keer what folks in the mountains say? I reckon ye mean as how they air a-talkin' about me

That's what I mean," said the mountaineer-" you 'n' him."

"Whut air they a-sayin'?" she asked, defiantly. Raines watched her narrowly.

"They air a-sayin' as how he air a-comin' up here mighty often; as how Easter Hicks, who hev never keered fer no man, air in love with this furriner from the settlemints."

The girl reddened, in spite of her assumed indifference.

"They- say, too, as how he air not in love with her, 'n' that somebody oughter warn Easter that he air not a-meanin' good to her. You hev been seed a-walkin' in the mountains together."

"Who seed me? " she asked, with quick suspicion. The mountaineer hesitated.

I hev," he said, doggedly.

The girl's anger, which had been kindling against her gossiping fellows, blazed out against Raines.

You've been watchin' me," she said, angrily. "Who give ye the right to do it? What call hev ye to come hyar and tell me whut folks is asayin'? Is it any o' yo' business? I want to tell ye, Sherd Raines"-her utterance grew thick-" that I kin take keer o' myself; that I don't keer what folks say; 'n' I want ye to keep away from me. 'N' ef I sees ye a-hangin' round 'n' a-spyin', ye'll be sorry fer it." Her eyes blazed, she had risen and drawn herself straight, and her hands were clinched.

The mountaineer stood motionless. " Thar's another who's seed ye," he said, quietly-" up thar," pointing to a wooded mountain, the top of which was lost in mist. The girl's attitude changed instantly into - vague alarm, and her eyes flashed upon Raines as though they would sear their way into the meaning hidden in his quiet face. Gradually his motive seemed to become clear, and she advanced a step toward him.

"So you've found out whar dad is a-hidin'?" she said, her voice tremulous with rage and scorn. N' ye air mean and sorry enough to some hyeh 'n' tell me ye'll give him up to the law ef I don't knuckle down 'n' do what ye wants me?

She paused a moment. Was her suspicion correct? Why did he not speak? She did not really believe what she said. Could it be true? Her nostrils quivered; she tried to speak again, but her voice was choked with passion. With a sudden movement she snatched her rifle from its place, and the steel flashed in the moonlight and ceased in a shining line straight at the mountaineer's breast.

"Look hyeh, Sherd Raines," she said, in low, unsteady tones, " I know you air religious, 'n' I know as how, when y'u give yer word, you'll do what you say. Now,

I want ye to hold up yer right hand and sw'ar that you'll never tell a livin' soul that you know whar dad is a-hidin'."

Raines did not turn his face, which was as emotionless as stone.

Air ye goin' to sw'ar? " she asked, with fierce impatience. Without looking at her, he began to speak-very slowly:

"Do ye think I'm fool enough to try to gain yer good-will by a-tellin' on yer dad? We were on the mountains, him 'n' me, we seed you 'n' the furriner. Yer dad thought hit was a spy, 'n' he whipped up his gun 'n' would 'a' shot him dead in his tracks ef I hadn't hindered him.

Does that look like I wanted to hurt the 'furriner? I hev knowed yer dad was up in the mountains all the time, 'n' I hev been a-totin' things fer him to eat. Does that look like I wanted to hand him over to the law?"

The girl had let the rifle fall. Moving away, she stood leaning on it in the shadow, looking down.

"You want to know what call I hev to watch ye, 'n' see that no harm comes to ye. Yer dad give me the right. You know how he hates furriners, 'n' whut he would do ef he happened to run across this furriner atter he has been drinkin'. I'm a-meddlin' because I hev told him that I am goin' to take keer o' ye, 'n' I mean to do it-ef ye hates me fer it. I'm a-watchin' ye, Easter," he continued, " 'n' I want ye to know it. I knowed the furriner begun comm' here cause ye air not like gals in the settlemints. Y'u air as cur'us to him as one o' them bugs an' sich-like that he's always a-pickin' up in the woods. I hevn't said nuthin' to yer dad, fer fear o' his harmin' the furriner; but I hev seed that ye like him, an' hit's time now fer me to meddle. Ef he was in love with ye, do ye think he would marry ye? I hev been in the settlemints. Folks thar air not as we citizens air. They air bigoted 'n' high-heeled, 'n' they look down on us. I tell ye, too- 'n' hit air fer yer own good-he air in love with somebody in the settlemints. I hev heerd it, 'n' I hev seed him a-lookin' at a picter in his room ez a man don't look at his sister. They say hit's her.

"Thar's one thing more, Easter," he concluded, as he stepped from the porch. "He is a-goin' away. I heard him say it yestiddy. What will ye do when he's gone ef ye lets yerself git to thinkin' so much of him now? I've warned ye now, Easter, fer yer own good, though ye mought think I'm a-workin' fer myself. But I know I hev done whut I ought. I've warned ye, 'n' ye kin do whut ye please, but I'm a-watchin' ye."

The girl said nothing, but stood rigid, with eyes wide open and face tense, as the mountaineer's steps died away. She was bewildered by the confused emotions that swayed her. Why had she not indignantly denied that she was in love with the "furriner"? Raines had not hinted it as a suspicion. He had spoken it outright as a fact, and he must have thought that her silence confirmed it. He had said that the "furriner" cared nothing for her, and had dared to tell her that she was in love with him. Her cheeks began to bum. She would call him back and tell him that she cared no more for the "furriner " than she did for him. She started from the steps, but paused, straining her eyes through the darkness. It was too late, and, with a helpless little cry, she began pacing the porch. She had scarcely heard what was said after the mountaineer's first accusation, so completely had that enthralled her mind; now fragments came back to her. There was something about a picture-ah! she remembered that picture. Passing through the camp one afternoon, she had glanced in at a window and had seen a rifle once her own. Turning in rapid wonder about the room, her eye lighted upon a picture on a table near the window. She had felt the refined beauty of the girl, and it had impressed her with the same timidity that Clayton had when she first knew him. Fascinated, she had looked till a - movement in the room made her shrink away. But the face had clung in her memory ever since, and now it came before her vividly. Clayton was in love with her. Well, what did that matter to her?

There was more that Raines said. "Goin' away." Raines meant the " furriner," of course. How did he know? Why had Clayton not told her? She did not believe it. But why not? He had once told her that he would go away some time; why not now? But why-why did not Clayton tell her? Perhaps he was going to her. She almost stretched out her hands in a sudden, fierce desire to clutch the round throat and sink her nails into the soft flesh that rose before her mind. She had forgotten that he had ever told her that he must go away, so little had it impressed her at the time. She had never thought of a possible change in their relations or in their lives. She tried to think what her life would be after he was gone, and she was frightened; she could not imagine her old life resumed. When Clayton came, it was as though she had risen from sleep in a dream, and had lived in it thereafter without questioning its reality. Into his hands she had delivered her life and herself with the undoubting faith of a child. She had never thought of their relations at all. Now the awakening had come. The dream was shattered. For the first time her eye was turned inward, where a flood of light brought into terrible distinctness the tumult that began to rage so suddenly within.

One hope only flashed into her brain-perhaps Raines was mistaken. But even then, if he were, Clayton must go some time; he had told her that. On this fact every thought became centred. It was no longer how he came, the richness of the new life he had shown her, the barrenness of the old, Raines's accusation, the shame of it-the shame of being pointed out and laughed at after Clayton's departure; it was no longer helpless wonder at the fierce emotions racking her for the first time: her whole being was absorbed in the realization which slowly forced itself into her heart and brain-some day he must go away; some day she must lose him. She lifted her hands to her head in a dazed, ineffectual way. The moonlight grew faint before her eyes; mountain, sky, and mist were in-distinguishably blurred; and the girl sank down upon her trembling knees, down till she lay crouched on the floor with her tearless face in her arms.

The moon rose high above her and sank down the west. The shadows shortened and crept back to the woods, night noises grew fainter, and the mists floated up from the valley and Clung around the mountain-tops; but she stirred only when a querulous voice came from within the cabin.

"Easter," it said, " ef Sherd Raines air gone, y'u better come in to bed. Y'u've got a lot o' work to do to-morrer."

The voice called her to the homely duties that had once filled her life and must fill it again. It was a summons to begin anew a life that was dead, and the girl lifted her haggard face in answer and rose wearily.

VII

ON the following Sunday morning, when Clayton walked up to the cabin, Easter and her mother were seated in the porch. He called to them cheerily as he climbed over the fence, but only the mother answered. Easter rose as he approached, and, without speaking, went within doors. He thought she must be ill, so thin and drawn was her face, but her mother said, carelessly:

Oh, hit's only one o' Easter's spells. She's been sort o' puny 'n' triflin' o' late, but I reckon she'll be all right ag'in in a day or two."

As the girl did not appear again, Clayton concluded that she was lying down, and went away without seeing her. Her manner had seemed a little odd, but, attributing that to ill-ness, he thought nothing further about it. To his surprise, the incident was repeated, and thereafter, to his wonder, the girl seemed to avoid him. Their intimacy was broken sharply off. When Clayton was at the cabin, either she did not appear or else kept herself busied with household duties. Their studies ceased abruptly. Easter had thrown her books into a corner, her mother said, and did nothing but mope all day; and though she insisted that it was only one of the girl's " spells," it was plain that something was wrong. Easter's face remained thin and drawn, and acquired gradually a hard, dogged, almost sullen look. She spoke to Clayton rarely, and then only in monosyllables. She never looked him in the face, and if his gaze rested intently on her, as she sat with eyes downcast and hands folded, she seemed to know it at once. Her face would color faintly, her hands fold and unfold nervously, and sometimes she would rise and go within. He had no opportunity of speaking with her alone. She seemed to guard against that, and, indeed, Raines's presence almost prevented it, for the mountaineer was there always, and always now the last to leave. He sat usually in the shadow of the vine, and though his-face was unseen, Clayton could feel his eyes fixed upon him with an intensity that sometimes made him nervous. The mountaineer had evidently begun to misinterpret his visits to the cabin. Clayton was regarded as a rival. In what other light, indeed, could he appear to Raines? Friendly calls between young people of opposite sex were rare in the mountains. When a young man visited a young woman, his intentions were supposed to be serious. Raines was plainly jealous.

But Easter? What was 'the reason for her odd behavior? Could she, too, have misconstrued his intentions as Raines had? It was impossible. But even if she had, his manner had in no wise changed. Some one else had aroused her suspicions, and if any one it must have been Raines. It was not the mother, he felt sure.

For some time Clayton's mother and sister had been urging him to make a visit home. He had asked leave of absence, but it was a busy time, and he had delayed indefinitely. In a fort-night, however, the stress of work would be over, and then he meant to leave. During that fortnight he was strangely troubled. He did not leave the camp, but his mind was busied with thoughts of Easter-nothing but Easter. Time and again he had reviewed their acquaintance minutely from the beginning, but he could find no cause for the change in her. When his work was done, he found himself climbing the mountain once more. He meant to solve the mystery if possible. He would tell Easter that he was going home. Surely she would betray some feeling then.

At the old fence which he had climbed so often he stopped, as was his custom, to rest a moment, with his eyes on the wild beauty before him-the great valley, with mists floating from its gloomy depths into the tremulous moonlight; far through the radiant space the still, dark masses of the Cumberland lifted in majesty against the east; and in the shadow of the great cliff the vague outlines of the old cabin, as still as the awful silence around it. A light was visible, but he could hear no voices. Still, he knew he would find the occupants seated in the porch, held by that strange quiet which nature imposes on those who dwell much alone with her. He had not been to the cabin for several weeks, and when he spoke Easter did not return his greeting; Raines nodded almost surlily, but from the mother came, as always, a cordial welcome.

"I'm mighty glad to see ye," she said; "you haven't been up fer a long time."

No," answered Clayton; "I have been very busy-getting ready to go home." He had watched Easter closely as he spoke, but the girl did not lift her face, and she betrayed no emotion, not even surprise; nor did Raines. Only the mother showed genuine regret. The girl's apathy filled him with bitter disappointment. She had relapsed into barbarism again. He was a fool to think that in a few months he could counteract influences that had been moulding her character for a century. His purpose had been unselfish. Curiosity, the girl's beauty, his increasing power over her, had stimulated him, to be sure, but he had been conscientious and earnest. Somehow he was more than disappointed; he was hurt deeply, not only that he should have been so misunderstood, but for the lack of gratitude in the girl. He was bewildered. What could have happened? Could Raines really have poisoned her mind against him? Would Easter so easily believe what might have been said against him and not allow him a hearing?

"I've been expecting to take a trip home for several weeks," he found himself saying a moment later; "I think I shall go to-morrow."

He hardly meant what he said; a momentary pique had forced the words from him, but, once spoken, he determined to abide by them. Easter was stirred from her lethargy at last, but Clayton's attention was drawn to Raines 's start of surprise, and he did not see the girl's face agitated for an instant, nor her hands nervously trembling in her lap.

"Ter-morrer! " cried the old woman. "Why, ye 'most take my breath away. I declar', I'm downright sorry you're goin', I hev tuk sech a shine to ye. I kind o' think I'll miss ye more'n Easter."

Raines's eyes turned to the girl, as did Clay-ton's. Not a suggestion of color disturbed the pallor of the girl's face, once more composed, and she said nothing.

You're so jolly 'n' lively," continued the mother, 'n' ye allus hev so much to say. You air not like Easter 'n' Sherd hyar, who talk 'bout as much as two stumps. I suppose I'll hev to sit up 'n' talk to the moon when you air gone."

The mountaineer rose abruptly, and, though he spoke quietly, he could hardly control himself.

"Ez my company seems to be unwelcome to ye," he said, "I kin take it away from ye, 'n' I will."

Before the old woman could recover herself, he was gone.

Well," she ejaculated, " whut kin be the matter with She rd? He hev got mighty cur'us hyar of late, 'n' so hev Easter. All o' ye been a-settin' up hyar ez ef you was at a buryin'. I'm a-goin' to bed. You 'n' Easter kin set up long as ye please. I suppose you air comm' back ag'in to see us," she said, turning to Clayton.

"I don't know," he answered. "I may not; but I sha'n't forget you."

"Well, I wish ye good luck." Clayton shook hands with her, and she went within doors.

The girl had risen, too, with her mother, and was standing in the shadow.

"Good-by Easter," said Clayton, holding out his hand.

As she turned he caught one glimpse of her face in the moonlight, and its whiteness startled him. Her hand was cold when he took it, and her voice was scarcely audible as she faintly repeated his words. She lifted her face as their hands were unclasped, and her lips quivered mutely as if trying to speak, but he had turned to go. For a moment she watched his darkening figure, and then with stifled breath almost staggered into the cabin.

The road wound around the cliff and back again, and as Clayton picked his way along it he was oppressed by a strange uneasiness. Easter's face, as he last saw it, lay in his mind like a keen reproach. Could he have been mistaken? Had he been too hasty? He recalled the events of the evening. He began to see that it was significant that Raines had shown no surprise when he spoke of going home, and yet had seemed almost startled by the suddenness of his departure. Perhaps the mountaineer knew he was going. It was known at the camp. If he knew, then Easter must have known. Perhaps she had felt hurt because he had not spoken to her earlier. What might Raines not have told her, and honestly, too? Perhaps he was unconsciously confirming all the mountaineer might have said. He ought to have spoken to her. Perhaps she could not speak to him. He wheeled suddenly in the path to return to the cabin, and stopped still.

Something was hurrying down through the undergrowth of the cliffside which towered darkly behind him. Nearer and nearer the bushes crackled as though some hunted animal were flying for life through them, and then through the laurel-hedge burst the figure of a woman, who sank to the ground in the path be-fore him. The flash of yellow hair and a white face in the moonlight told him who it was.

"Easter, Easter! " he exclaimed, in sickening fear. "My God! is that you? Why, what is the matter, child? What are you doing here?"

He stooped above the sobbing girl, and pulled away her hands from her face, tear-stained and broken with pain. The limit of her self-repression was reached at last; the tense nerves, strained too much, had broken; and the passion, so long checked, surged through her like fire. Ah, God! what had he done? He saw the truth at last. In an impulse of tenderness he lifted the girl to her feet and held her, sobbing uncontrollably, in his arms, with her head against his breast, and his cheek on her hair, soothing her as though she had been a child.

Presently she felt a kiss on her forehead. She looked up with a sudden fierce joy in her eyes, and their lips met.

VIII

CLAYTON shunned all self-questioning after that night. Stirred to the depths by that embrace on the mountain-side, he gave himself wholly up to the love or infatuation-he did not ask which-that enthralled him. Whatever it was, its growth had been subtle and swift. There was in it the thrill that might come from taming some wild creature that had never known control, and the gentleness that to any generous spirit such power would bring. These, with the magnetism of the girl's beauty and personality, and the influence of her environment, he had felt for a long time; but now richer chords were set vibrating in response to her great love, the struggle she had against its disclosure, the appeal for tenderness and protection in her final defeat. It was ideal, he told himself, as he sank into the delicious dream; they two alone with nature, above all human life, with its restraints, its hardships, its evils, its distress. For them was the freedom of the open sky lifting its dome above the mountains; for them nothing less kindly than the sun shining its benediction; for their eyes only the changing beauties of day and night; for their ears no sound harsher than the dripping of dew or a bird-song; for them youth, health, beauty, love. And it was primeval love, the love of the first woman for the first man. She knew no convention, no prudery, no doubt. Her life was impulse, and her impulse was love. She was the teacher now, and he the taught; and he stood in wonder when the plant he had tended flowered into such beauty in a single night. Ah, the happy, happy days that followed! The veil that had for a long time been unfolding itself between him and his previous life seemed to have almost fallen, and they were left alone to their happiness. The mother kept her own counsel. Raines had disappeared as though Death had claimed him. And the dream lasted till a summons home broke into it as the sudden flaring up of a candle will shatter a reverie at twilight.

IX

THE summons was from his father, and was emphatic; and Clayton did not delay. The girl accepted his departure with a pale face, but with a quiet submission that touched him. Of Raines he had seen nothing and heard nothing since the night he had left the cabin in anger; but as he came down the mountain after bidding Easter good-by, he was startled by the mountaineer stepping from the bushes into the path.

Ye air a-goin' home, I hear," he said, quietly.

"Yes," answered Clayton; " at midnight."

Well, I'll walk down with ye a piece, ef ye don't mind. Hit's not out o' my way."

As he spoke his face was turned suddenly to the moonlight. The lines in it had sunk deeper, giving it almost an aged look; the eyes were hollow as from physical suffering or from fasting. He preceded Clayton down the path, with head bent, and saying nothing till they reached the spur of the mountain. Then in the same voice:

"I want to talk to ye awhile, 'n' I'd like to hev ye step inter my house. I don't mean ye no harm," he added, quickly, " 'n' hit ain't fer."

Certainly," said Clayton.

The mountaineer turned into the woods by a narrow path, and soon the outlines of a miserable little hut were visible through the dark woods. Raines thrust the door open. The single room was dark except for a few dull coals in a gloomy cavern which formed the fireplace.

Sit down, ef ye kin find a cheer," said Raines, " 'n' I'll fix up the fire."

Do you live here alone?" asked Clayton. He could hear the keen, smooth sound of the mountaineer's knife going through wood.

"Yes," he answered; " fer five year."

The coals brightened; tiny flames shot from them; in a moment the blaze caught the dry fagots, and shadows danced over the floor, wall, and ceiling, and vanished as the mountaineer rose from his knees. The room was as bare as the cell of a monk. A rough bed stood in one corner; a few utensils hung near the fireplace, wherein were remnants of potatoes roasting in the ashes, and close to the wooden shutter which served as a window was a board table. On it lay a large book-a Bible-a pen, a bottle of ink, and a piece of paper on which were letters traced with great care and difficulty. The mountaineer did not sit down, but began pacing the floor behind Clayton. Clayton moved his chair, and Raines seemed unconscious of his presence as with eyes on the floor he traversed the narrow width of the cabin.

Y'u hevn't seed me up on the mount 'in lately, hev ye? " he asked. "I reckon ye haven't missed me much. Do ye know whut I've been doin'?" he said, with sudden vehemence, stopping still and resting his eyes, which glowed like an animal's from the darkened end of the cabin, on Clayton.

"I've been tryin' to keep from killin' ye. Oh, don't move-don't fear now; ye air as safe as ef ye were down in the camp. I seed ye that night on the mount'in," he continued, pacing rapidly back and forth. "I was waitin' fer ye. I meant to tell ye jest whut I'm goin' to tell ye ter-night; 'n' when Easter come a-tearin' through the bushes, 'n' I seed ye-ye-a-standin' together "-the words seemed to stop in his throat-" I knowed I was too late.

"I sot thar fer a minute like a rock, 'n' when ye two went back up the mount'in, before I knowed it I was hyer in the house thar at the fire mouldin' a bullet to kill ye with as ye come back. All at oncet I heerd a voice plain as my own is at this minute:

"'Air you a-thinkin' 'bout takin' the life of a fellow-creatur, Sherd Raines-you that air tryin' to be a servant o' the Lord?'"

"But I kept on a-mouldin', 'n' suddenly I seed ye a-layin' in the road dead, 'n' the heavens opened 'n' the face o' the Lord was thar, 'n' he raised his hand to smite me with the brand o' Cain-'n' look thar!"

Clayton had sat spellbound by the terrible earnestness of the man, and as the mountaineer swept his dark hair back with one hand, he rose in sudden horror. Across the mountaineer's forehead ran a crimson scar yet unhealed. Could he have inflicted upon himself this fearful penance?

Oh, it was only the moulds. I seed it all so plain that I throwed up my hands, fergittin' the moulds, 'n' the hot lead struck me thar; but," he continued, solemnly, "I knowed the Lord hed tuk that way o' punishin' me fer the sin o havin' murder in my mind, 'n' I fell on my knees right thar a-prayin' fer fergiveness: 'n' since that night I hev stayed away from ye till the Lord give me power to stand ag'in the temptation o' harmin' ye. He hev showed me another way, 'n' now I hev come to ye as he hev tol' me. I hevn't tol' ye this fer nothin'. Y'u in see now whut I think o' Easter, ef I was tempted to take the life o' the man who tuk her from me, 'n' I reckon ye will say I've got the right to ax ye whut I'm a-goin' to. I hev knowed the gal sence she was a baby. We was children together, and thar hain't no use hidin' that I never keered a straw fer anuther woman. She used to be mighty wilful 'n' contrary, but as soon as you come I seed at oncet that a change was comm' over her. I mistrusted ye, 'n' I warned her ag'in' ye. But when I l'arned that ye was a-teachin' her, and a-doin' whut I had tried my best to do 'n' failed, I let things run along, thinkin' that mebbe ever'thing would come out right, after all. Mebbe hit air all right, but I come to ye now, 'n' I ax ye in the name of the livin' God, who is a-watchin' you a-guidin' me, air ye goin' to leave the po' gal to die sorrowin' fer ye, or do ye aim to come back 'n' marry her?

Raines had stopped now in the centre of the cabin, and the shadows flickering slowly over him gave an unearthly aspect to his tall, gaunt figure, as he stood with uplifted arm, pale face, glowing eyes, and disordered hair.

"The gal hasn't got no protecter-her dad, as you know, is a-hidin' from jestice in the mount'ins-and I'm a-standin' in his place, 'n' I ax ye to do only whut you know ye ought."

There was nothing threatening in the mountaineer 's attitude, nor dictatorial; and Clayton felt his right to say what he had, in spite of a natural impulse to resent such interference. Besides, there sprang up in his heart a sudden great admiration for this rough, uncouth fellow who was capable of such unselfishness; who, true to the trust of her father and his God, was putting aside the strongest passion of his life for what he believed was the happiness of the woman who had inspired it. He saw, too, that the sacrifice was made with perfect unconsciousness that it was unusual or admirable. He rose to his feet, and the two men faced each other.

"If you had told me this long ago," said Clayton, "I should have gone away, but you seemed distrustful and suspicious. I did not expect the present state of affairs to come about, but since it has, I tell you frankly that I have never thought of doing anything else than what you have asked."

And he told the truth, for he had already asked himself that question. Why should he not marry her? He must in all probability stay in the mountains for years, and after that time he would not be ashamed to take her home, so strong was his belief in her quickness and adaptibility.

Raines seemed scarcely to believe what he heard. He had not expected such ready acquiescence. He had almost begun to fear from Clayton's silence that he was going to refuse, and then-God knows what he would have done.

Instantly he stretched out his hand.

"I hev done ye great wrong, 'n' I ax yer par-din," he said, huskily. "I want to say that I bear ye no gredge, 'n' thet I wish ye well. I hope ye won't think hard on me," he continued; "I he had a hard fight with the devil as long as I can ricolect. I hev turned back time 'n' ag'in, but thar hain't nothin' ter keep me from goin' straight ahead now."

As Clayton left the cabin, the mountaineer stopped him for a moment on the threshold.

"Thar's another thing I reckon I ought to tell ye," he said; " Easter's dad air powerfully sot ag'in ye. He thought ye was an officer at fust, 'n' hit was hard to git him out o' the idee thet ye was spyin' fer him; 'n' when he seed ye goin' to the house, he got it inter his head that ye mought be meanin' harm to Easter, who air the only thing alive thet he keers fer much. He promised not to tech ye, 'n' I knowed he would keep his word as long as he was sober. It'll be all right now, I reckon," he concluded, "when I tell him whut ye aims to do, though he hev got a spite ag'in all furriners. Far'well! I wish ye well; I wish ye well."

An hour later Clayton was in Jellico. It was midnight when the train came in, and he went immediately to his berth. Striking the curtain accidentally, he loosed it from its fastenings, and, doubling the pillows, he lay looking out on the swiftly passing landscape. The moon was full and brilliant, and there was a strange, keen pleasure in being whirled in such comfort through the night. The mists almost hid the mountains. They seemed very, very far away. A red star trembled in the crest of

Wolf Mountain. Easter's cabin must be almost under that Star. He wondered if she were asleep. Perhaps she was out on the porch, lonely, suffering, and thinking of him. He felt her kiss and her tears upon his hand. Did he not love her? Could there be any doubt about that? His thoughts turned toRaines, and he saw the mountaineer in his lonely cabin, sitting with his head bowed in his hands in front of the dying fire. He closed his eyes, and another picture rose before him-a scene at home. He had taken Easter to New York. How brilliant the light! what warmth and luxury! There stood his father, there his mother. What gracious dignity they had! Here was his sister-what beauty and elegance and grace of manner! But Easter! Wherever she was placed the other figures needed readjustment. There was something irritably incongruous-Ah! now he had it-his mind grew hazy-he was asleep.

X

DURING the weeks that followed, some malignant spirit seemed to be torturing him with a slow realization of all he had lost; taunting him with the possibility of regaining it and the certainty of losing it forever. As he stepped from the dock at Jersey City the fresh sea wind had thrilled him like a memory, and his pulses leaped instantly into sympathy with the tense life that vibrated in the air. He seemed never to have been away so long, and never had home seemed so pleasant. His sister had grown more beautiful; his mother's quiet, noble face was smoother and fairer than it had been for years; and despite the absence of his father, who had been hastily summoned to England, there was an air of cheerfulness in the house that was in marked contrast to its gloom when Clayton was last at home. He had been quickened at once into a new appreciation of the luxury and refinement about him, and he soon began to wonder how he had inured himself to the discomforts and crudities of his mountain life. Old habits easily resumed sway over him. At the club friend and acquaintance were so unfeignedly glad to see him that he began to suspect that his own inner gloom had darkened their faces after his father's misfortune. Day after day found him in his favorite corner at the club, watching the passing pageant and listening eagerly to the conversational froth of the town-the gossip of club, theatre, and society. His ascetic life in the mountains gave to every pleasure the taste of inexperience. His early youth seemed renewed, so keen and fresh were his emotions. He felt, too, that he was recovering a lost identity, and still the new one that had grown around him would not loosen its hold. He had told his family nothing of Easter-why, he could scarcely have said-and the difficulty of telling increased each day. His secret began to weigh heavily upon him; and though he determined to unburden himself on his father's return, he was troubled with a vague sense of deception. When he went to receptions with his sister, this sense of a double identity was keenly felt amid the lights, the music, the flowers, the flash of eyes and white necks and arms, the low voices, the polite, clear-cut utterances of welcome and compliment.

Several times he had met a face for which he had once had a boyish infatuation. Its image had never been supplanted during his student career, but he had turned from it as from a star when he came home and found that his life was to be built with his own hands. Now the girl had grown to gracious womanhood, and when he saw her he was thrilled with the remembrance that she had once favored him above all others. One night a desire assailed him to learn upon what footing he then stood. He had yielded, and she gave him a kindly welcome. They had drifted to reminiscence, and Clayton went home that night troubled at heart and angry that he should be so easily disturbed; surprised that the days were passing so swiftly, and pained that they were filled less and less with thoughts of Easter. With a pang of remorse and fear, he determined to go back to the mountains as soon as his father came home. He knew the effect of habit. He would forget these pleasures felt so keenly now, as he had once forgotten them, and he would leave before their hold upon him was secure.

Knowing the danger that beset him, Puritan that he was, he had avoided it all he could. He even stopped his daily visits to the club, and spent most of his time at home with his mother and sister. Once only, to his bitter regret, was he induced to go out. Wagner's tidal wave had reached New York; it was the opening night of the season, and the opera was one that he had learned to love in Germany. The very brilliancy of the scene threw him into gloom, so aloof did he feel from it all-the great theatre aflame with lights, the circling tiers of faces, the pit with its hundred musicians, their eyes on the leader, who stood above them with baton upraised and German face already aglow.

In his student days he had loved music, but he had little more than trifled with it; now, strangely enough, his love, even his understanding, seemed to have grown; and when the violins thrilled all the vast space into life, he was shaken with a passion newly born. All the evening he sat riveted. A rush of memories came upon him-memories of his student life, with its dreams and ideals of culture and scholarship, which rose from his past again like phantoms. In the elevation of the moment the trivial pleasures that had been tempting him became mean and unworthy. With a pang of bitter regret he saw himself as he might have been, as he yet might be.

A few days later his father came home, and his distress of mind was complete. Clayton need stay in the mountains but little longer, he said; he was fast making up his losses, and he had hoped after his trip to England to have Clayton at once in New York; but now he had best wait perhaps another year. Then had come a struggle that racked heart and brain. All he had ever had was before him again. Could it be his duty to shut himself from this life-his natural heritage-to stifle the highest demands of his nature? Was he seriously in love with that mountain girl? Had he indeed ever been sure of himself? If, then, he did not love her beyond all question, would he not wrong himself, wrong her, by marrying her? Ah, but might he not wrong her, wrong himself -even more? He was bound to her by every tie that his sensitive honor recognized among the duties of one human being to another. He had sought her; he had lifted her above her own life. If one human being had ever put its happiness in the hands of another, that had been done. If he had not deliberately taught her to love him, he had not tried to prevent it. He could not excuse himself; the thought of gaining her affection had occurred to him, and he had put it aside. There was no excuse; for when she gave her love, he had accepted it, and, as far as she knew, had given his own unreservedly. Ah, that fatal moment of weakness, that night on the mountam-side! Could he tell her, could he tell Raines, the truth, and ask to be released? What could Easter with her devotion, and Raines with his singleness of heart, know of this substitute for love which civilization had taught him? Or, granting that they could understand, he might return home; but Easter-what was left for her?

It was useless to try to persuade himself that her love would fade away, perhaps quickly, and leave no scar; that Raines would in time win her for himself, his first idea of their union be realized, and, in the end, all happen for the best. That might easily be possible with a different nature under different conditions-a nature less passionate, in contact with the world and responsive to varied interests; but not with Easter -alone with a love that had shamed him, with mountain, earth, and sky unchanged, and the vacant days marked only by a dreary round of wearisome tasks. He remembered Raines s last words-" Air ye goin' to leave the po' gal to die sorrowin' fer ye ? " What happiness would be possible for him with that lonely mountain-top and the white, drawn face forever haunting him?

That very night a letter came, with a rude superscription-the first from Easter. Within it was a poor tintype, from which Easter's eyes looked shyly at him. Before he left he had tried in vain to get her to the tent of an itinerant photographer. During his absence, she had evidently gone of her own accord. The face was very beautiful, and in it was an expression of questioning, modest pride. "Aren't you surprised? "it seemed to say-" and pleased? Only the face, with its delicate lines, and the throat and the shoulders were visible. She looked almost refined. And the note-it was badly spelled and written with great difficulty, but it touched him. She was lonely, she said, and she wanted him to come back. Lonely- that cry was in each line.

His response to this was an instant resolution to go back at once, and, sensitive and pliant as his nature was, there was no hesitation for him when his duty was clear and a decision once made. With great care and perfect frankness he had traced the history of his infatuation in a letter to his father, to be communicated when the latter chose to his mother and sister. Now he was nearing the mountains again.

XI

THE journey to the mountains was made with a heavy heart. In his absence everything seemed to have suffered a change. Jellico had never seemed so small, so coarse, so wretched as when he stepped from the dusty train and saw it lying dwarfed and shapeless in the afternoon sunlight. The State line bisects the straggling streets of frame-houses. On the Kentucky side an extraordinary spasm of morality had quieted into local option. Just across the way in Tennessee was a row of saloons. It was "pay-day" for the miners, and the worst element of all the mines was drifting in to spend the following Sabbath in unchecked vice. Several rough, brawny fellows were already staggering from Tennessee into Kentucky, and around one saloon hung a crowd of slatternly negroes, men and women. Heartsick with disgust, Clayton hurried into the lane that wound through the valley. Were these hovels, he asked himself in wonder, the cabins he once thought so poetic, so picturesque? How was it that they suggested now only a pitiable poverty of life? From each, as he passed, came a rough, cordial shout of greeting. Why was he jarred so strangely? Even nature had changed. The mountains seemed stunted, less beautiful. The light, streaming through the western gap with all the splendor of a mountain sunset, no longer thrilled him. The moist fragrance of the earth at twilight, the sad pipings of birds by the wayside, the faint, clear notes of a wood-thrush-his favorite-from the edge of the forest, even the mid-air song of a meadow-lark above his head, were unheeded as, with face haggard with thought and travel, he turned doggedly from the road and up the mountain toward Easter's home. The novelty and ethnological zeal that had blinded him to the disagreeable phases of mountain life were gone; so was the pedestal from which he had descended to make a closer study of the people. For he felt now that he had gone among them with an unconscious condescension; his interest seemed now to have been little more than curiosity-a pastime to escape brooding over his own change of fortune. And with Easter-ah, how painfully clear his mental vision had grown! Was it the tragedy of wasting possibilities that had drawn him to her-to help her-or was it his own miserable selfishness, after all?

No one was visible when he reached the cabin. The calm of mountain and sky enthralled it as completely as the cliff that towered behind it. The day still lingered, and the sunlight rested lightly on each neighboring crest. As he stepped upon the porch there was a slight noise within the cabin, and, peering into the dark interior, he called Easter's name. There was no answer, and he sank wearily into a chair, his thoughts reverting homeward. By this time his mother and sister must know why he had come back to the mountains. He could imagine their consternation and grief. Perhaps that was only the beginning; he might be on the eve of causing them endless unhappiness. He had thought to involve them as little as possible by remaining in the mountains; but the thought of living there was now intolerable in the new relations he would sustain to the people. What should he do? where go? As he bent fQrward in perplexity, there was a noise again in the cabin-this time the stealthy tread of feet-and before he could turn, a rough voice vibrated threateningly in his ears:

Say who ye air, and what yer business is, mighty quick, er ye hain't got a minute to live."

Clayton looked up, and to his horror saw the muzzle of a rifle pointed straight at his head. At the other end of it, and standing in the door, was a short, stocky figure, a head of bushy hair, and a pair of small, crafty eyes. The fierceness and suddenness of the voice, in the great silence about him, and its terrible earnestness, left him almost paralyzed.

"Come, who air ye? Say quick, and don't move, nother"

Clayton spoke his name with difficulty. The butt of the rifle dropped to the floor, and with a harsh laugh its holder advanced to him with hand outstretched:

So ye air Easter's feller, air ye? Well, I'm yer dad-that's to be. Shake."

Clayton shuddered. Good heavens! this was Easter's father! More than once or twice, his name had never been mentioned at the cabin.

I tuk ye fer a raider," continued the old mountaineer, not noticing Clayton's repulsion, "'n' ef ye had 'a' been, ye wouldn't be nobody now. I reckon Easter hain't told ye much about me, 'n' I reckon she hev a right to be a leetle ashamed of me. I had a leetle trouble down thar in the valley-I s'pose you've heerd about it-'n' I've had to keep kind o' quiet. I seed ye once afore, 'n' I come near shootin' ye, thinkin' ye was a raider. Am mighty glad I didn't, fer Easter is powerful sot on ye. Sherd thought I could resk comm' down to the wed-din'. They hev kind o' give up the s'arch, 'n' none o' the boys won't tell on me. We'll have an old-timer, I tell ye. Ye folks from the settle-mints air mighty high-heeled, but old Bill Hicks don't allus go bar'footed. He kin step purty high, 'n' he's a-goin' to do it at that weddin'. Hev somefin?" he asked, suddenly pulling out a flask of colorless liquid. "Ez ye air to be one o' the fambly, I don't mind tellin' ye thar's the very moonshine that caused the leetle trouble down in the valley."

For fear of giving offence, Clayton took a swallow of the liquid, which burned him like fire. He had scarcely recovered from the first shock, and he had listened to the man and watched him with a sort of enthralling fascination. He was Easter's father. He could even see a faint suggestion of Easter's face in the cast of the features before him, coarse and degraded as they were. He had the same nervous, impetuous quickness, and, horrified by the likeness, Clayton watched him sink back into a chair, pipe in mouth, and relapse into a stolidity that seemed incapable of the energy and fire shown scarcely a moment before. His life in the mountains had made him as shaggy as some wild animal. He was coatless, and his trousers of jeans were upheld by a single home-made suspender. His beard was yet scarcely touched with gray, and his black, lustreless hair fell from under a round hat of felt with ragged tdges and uncertain color. The mountaineer did not speak again until, with great deliberation and care, he had filled a cob pipe. Then he bent his sharp eyes upon Clayton so fixedly that the latter let his own fall.

"Mebbe ye don't know that I'm ag'in' fur-riners," he said, abruptly, " all o' ye; 'n' ef the Lord hisself hed 'a' tol' me thet my gal would be a-marryin' one, I wouldn't 'a' believed him. But Sherd hev told me ye air all right, 'n' ef Sherd says ye air, why, ye air, I reckon, 'n' I hevn't got nothin' to say; though I hev got a heap ag'in ye-all o' ye."

His voice had a hint of growing anger under the momentary sense of his wrongs, and, not wishing to incense him further, Clayton said nothing.

Ye air back a little sooner than ye expected, ain't ye? " he asked, presently, with an awkward effort at good-humor. "I reckon ye air gittin' anxious. Well, we hev been gittin' ready fer ye, 'n' you 'n' Easter kin hitch ez soon ez ye please. Sherd Raines air gum' to do the marryin'. He air the best friend I got. Sherd was a-courtin' the gal, too, but he hevn't got no gredge ag'in ye, 'n' he hev promised to tie ye. Sherd air a preacher now. He hev just got his license. He didn't want to do it, but I told him he had to. We'll hev the biggest weddin' ever seed in these mountains, I tell ye. Any o' yo' folks be on hand?"

No," answered Clayton, soberly, "I think not."

"Well, I reckon we kin fill up the house."

Clayton's heart sank at the ordeal of a wedding with such a master of ceremonies. He was about to ask where Easter and her mother were, when, to his relief, he saw them both in the path below, approaching the house. The girl was carrying a bucket of water on her head. Once he would have thought her picturesque, but now it pained him to see her doing such rough work. When she saw him, she gave a cry of surprise and delight that made Clayton tingle with remorse. Then running to him with glowing face, she stopped suddenly, and, with a look down at her bare feet and soiled gown, fled into the cabin. Clayton followed, but the room was so dark he could see nothing.

Easter! " he called. There was no answer, but he was suddenly seized about the neck by a pair of unseen arms and kissed by unseen lips twice in fierce succession, and before he could turn and clasp the girl she was laughing softly in the next room, with a barred door between them. Clayton waited patiently several minutes, and then asked:

Easter, aren't you ready?

Not yit-not yet!" She corrected herself with such vehemence that Clayton laughed. She came out presently, and blushed when Clayton looked her over from head to foot with astonishment. She was simply and prettily dressed in white muslin; a blue ribbon was about her throat, and her hair was gathered in a Psyche knot that accented the classicism of her profile. Her appearance was really refined and tasteful. When they went out on the porch he noticed that her hands had lost their tanned appearance. Her feet were slippered, and she wore black stockings. He remembered the book of fashion-plates he had once sent her; it was that that had quickened her instinct of dress. He said nothing, but the happy light in Easter's face shone brighter as she noted his pleased and puzzled gaze.

Why, ye look like another man," said Easter's mother, who had been looking Clayton over with a quizzical smile. "Is that the way folks dress out in the settlem-ints? 'N' look at that gal. Ef she hev done anythin' sence ye hev been gone but " The rest of the sentence was smothered in the palm of Easter's hand, and she too began scrutinizing Clayton closely. The mountaineer said nothing, and after a curi-ous glance at Easter resumed his pipe.

You look like a pair of butterflies," said the mother when released. "Sherd oughter be mighty proud of his first marryin'. I s'pose ye know he air a preacher now? Ye oughter heerd him preach last Sunday. It was his fust time. The way he lighted inter the furriners was a caution. He 'lowed he was a-goin' to fight cyard-playin' and dancin' ez long ez he hed breath."

Yes; 'n' thar's whar Sherd air a fool. I'm ag'in furriners, too, but thar hain't no harm in dancin, n' thar's goin' to be dancin' at this weddin' ef I'm alive."

Easter shrank perceptibly when her father spoke, and looked furtively at Clayton, who winced, in spite of himself, as the rough voice grated in his ear. Instantly her face grew unhappy, and contained an appeal for pardon that he was quick to understand and appreciate. Thereafter he concealed his repulsion, and treated the rough bear so affably that Easter's eyes grew moist with gratitude.

Darkness was gathering in the valley below when he rose to go. Easter had scarcely spoken to him, but her face and her eyes, fixed always upon him, were eloquent with joy. Once as she passed behind him her hand rested with a timid, caressing touch upon his shoulder, and now, as he walked away from the porch, she called him back. He turned, and she had gone into the house.

What is it, Easter? " he asked, stepping into the dark room. His hand was grasped in both her own and held tremblingly.

Don't mind dad," she whispered, softly. Something warm and moist fell upon his hand as she unloosed it, and she was gone.

That night he wrote home in a better frame of mind. The charm of the girl's personality had asserted its power again, and hopes that had almost been destroyed by his trip home were rekindled by her tasteful appearance, her delicacy of feel-ing, and by her beauty, which he had not overrated. He asked that his sister might meet him in Louisville after the wedding-whenever that should be. They two could decide then what should be done. His own idea was to travel; and so great was his confidence in Easter, he believed that, in time, he could take her to New York without fear.

XII

IT was plain that Raines-to quiet the old man's uneasiness, perhaps-had told him of his last meeting with Clayton, and that, during the absence of the latter, some arrangements for the wedding had been made, even by Easter, who in her trusting innocence had perhaps never thought of any other end to their relations. In consequence, there was an unprecedented stir among the mountaineers. The marriage of a citizen with a " furriner " was an unprecedented event, and the old mountaineer, who began to take some pride in the alliance, emphasized it at every opportunity.

At the mines Clayton's constant visits to the mountain were known to everybody, but little attention had been paid to them. Now, however, when the rumor of the wedding seemed confirmed by his return and his silence, every one was alert with a curiosity so frankly shown that he soon became eager to get away from the mountains. Accordingly, he made known his wish to Easter's parents that the marriage should take place as soon as possible. Both received the suggestion with silent assent. Then had followed many difficulties. Only as a great concession to the ideas and customs of " fur-riners" would the self-willed old mountaineer agree that the ceremony should take place at night, and that after the supper and the dance, the two should leave Jellico at daybreak. Mountain marriages were solemnized in the daytime, and wedding journeys were unknown. The old man did not understand why Clayton should wish to leave the mountains, and the haste of the latter seemed to give him great offence. When Clayton had ventured to suggest, instead, that the marriage should be quiet, and that he and Easter should remain on the mountain a few days before leaving, he fumed with anger; and thereafter any suggestion from the young engineer was met with a suspicion that looked ominous. Raines was away on his circuit, and would not return until just before the wedding, so that from him Clayton could get no help. Very wisely, then, he interfered no more, but awaited the day with dread.

It was nearing dusk when he left the camp on his wedding-night. Half-way up the mountain he stopped to lean against the kindly breast of a bowlder blocking the path. It was the spot where he had seen Easter for the first time. The mountains were green again, as they were then, but the scene seemed sadly changed. The sun was gone; the evening-star had swung its white light like a censer above Devil's Den; the clouds were moving swiftly through the darkening air, like a frightened flock seeking a fold; and the night was closing fast over the cluster of faint camp-fires. The spirit brooding over mountain and sky was unspeakably sad, and with a sharp pain at his heart Clayton turned from it and hurried on. Mountain, sky, and valley were soon lost in the night. When he reached the cabin rays of bright light were flashing from chink and crevice into the darkness, and from the kitchen came the sounds of busy preparation. Already many guests had arrived. A group of men who stood lazily talking in the porch became silent as he approached, but, recognizing none of them, he entered the cabin. A dozen women were seated about the room, and instantly their eyes were glued upon him. As the kitchen door swung open he saw Easter's mother bending over the fireplace, a table already heavily laden, and several women bustling about it. Above his head he heard laughter, a hurried tramping of feet, and occasional cries of surprise and delight. He paused at the threshold, hardly knowing what to do, and when he turned a titter from one corner showed that his embarrassment was seen. On the porch he was seized by Easter's father, who drew him back into the room. The old mountaineer's face was flushed, and he had been drinking heavily.

Oh, hyar ye air! " he exclaimed. "You're right on hand, hain't ye? Hyar, Bill," he called, thrusting his head out of the door, "you "n' Jim 'n' Milt come in hyar." Three awkward young mountaineers entered. "These fellers air goin' to help ye."

They were to be his ushers. Clayton shook hands with them gravely.

Oh, we air about ready fer ye, 'n' we air only waitin' fer Sherd and the folks to come," continued the mountaineer, jubilantly, winking significantly at Clayton and his attendants, who stood about him at the fireplace. Clayton shook his head firmly, but the rest followed Hicks, who turned at the door and repeated the invitation with a frowning face. Clayton was left the focus of feminine eyes, whose unwavering directness kept his own gaze on the floor. People began to come in rapidly, most of whom he had never seen before. The room was filled, save for a space about him. Every one gave him a look of curiosity that made him feel like some strange animal on exhibition. Once more he tried to escape to the porch, and again he was met by Easter's father, who this time was accompanied by Raines.

The young circuit-rider was smoothly shaven, and dressed in dark clothes, and his calm face and simple but impressive manner seemed at once to alter the atmosphere of the room. He grasped Clayton's hand warmly, and without a trace of self-consciousness. The room had grown instantly quiet, and Raines began to share the curious interest that Clayton had caused; for the young mountaineer's sermon had provoked discussion far and wide, and, moreover, the peculiar relations of the two toward Easter were known and rudely appreciated. Hicks was subdued into quiet respect, and tried to conceal his incipient intoxication. The effort did not last long. When the two fiddlers came, he led them in with a defiant air, and placed them in the corner, bustling about officiously but without looking at Raines, whose face began to cloud.

Well, we're all hyar, I reckon! " he exclaimed, in his terrible voice. "Is Easter ready? " he shouted up the steps.

A confused chorus answered him affirmatively, and he immediately arranged Clayton in one corner of the room with his serious attendants on one side, and Raines, grave to solemnity, on the other. Easter's mother and her assistants came in from the kitchen, and the doors were filled with faces. Above, the tramping of feet became more hurried; below, all stood with expectant faces turned to the rude staircase. Clayton's heart began to throb, and a strange light brightened under Raines's heavy brows.

"Hurry up, thar!" shouted Hicks, impatiently.

A moment later two pairs of rough shoes came down the steps, and after them two slippered feet that fixed every eye in the room, until the figure and face above them slowly descended into the light. Midway the girl paused with a timid air. Had an angel been lowered to mortal view, the waiting people would not have been stricken with more wonder. Raines's face relaxed into a look almost of awe, and even Hicks for the instant was stunned into reverence. Mountain eyes had never beheld such loveliness so arrayed. It was simple enough-the garment-all white, and of a misty texture, yet it formed a mysterious vision to them. About the girl's brow was a wreath of pink and white laurel. A veil had not been used. It would hide her face, she said, and she did not see why that should be done. For an instant she stood poised so lightly that she seemed to sway like a vision, as the candle-lights quivered about her, with her hands clasped in front of her, and her eyes wandering about the room till they lighted upon Clayton with a look of love that seemed to make her conscious only of him. Then, with quickening breath, lips parted slightly, cheeks slowly flushing, and shining eyes still upon him, she moved slowly across the room until she stood at his side.

Raines gathered himself together as from a dream, and stepped before the pair. Broken and husky at first, his voice trembled in spite of himself, but thereafter there was no hint of the powerful emotions at play within him. Only as he joined their hands, his eyes rested an instant with infinite tenderness on Easter's face-as though the look were a last farewell-and his voice deepened with solemn earnestness when he bade Clayton protect and cherish her until death. There was a strange mixture in those last words of the office and the man-of divine authority and personal appeal-and Clay. ton was deeply stirred. The benediction over4 the young preacher was turning away, when some one called huskily from the rear of the cabin:

"Whyn't ye kiss the bride?

It was Easter's father, and the voice, rough as it was, brought a sensation of relief to all. The young mountaineer's features contracted with swift pain, and as Easter leaned toward him, with subtle delicacy, he touched, not her lips, but her forehead, as reverently as though she had been a saint.

Instantly the fiddles began, the floor was cleared, the bridal party hurried into the kitchen, and the cabin began to shake beneath dancing feet. Hicks was fulfilling his word, and in the kitchen his wife had done her part. Everything known to the mountaineer palate was piled in profusion on the table, but Clayton and Easter ate nothing. To him the whole evening was a nightmare, which the solemn moments of the marriage had made the more hideous. He was restless and eager to get away. The dancing was becoming more furious, and above the noise rose Hicks's voice prompting the dancers. The ruder ones still hung about the doors, regarding Clayton curiously, or with eager eyes upon the feast. Easter was vaguely troubled, and conflicting with the innocent pride and joy in her eyes were the questioning glances she turned to Clayton's darkening face. At last they were hurried out, and in came the crowd like hungry wolves.

Placing Clayton and Easter in a corner of the room, the attendants themselves took part in the dancing, and such dancing Clayton had never seen. Doors and windows were full of faces, and the room was crowded; from the kitchen came coarse laughter and the rattling of dishes.

Occasionally Hicks would disappear with several others, and would return with his face redder than ever.

Easter became uneasy. Once she left Clayton's side and expostulated with her father, but he shook her from his arm roughly. Raines saw this, and a moment later he led the old mountaineer from the room. Thereafter the latter was quieter, but only for a little while. Several times the kitchen was filled and emptied, and ever was the crowd unsteadier. Soon even Raines's influence was of no avail, and the bottle was passed openly from guest to guest.

"Whyn't ye dance?"

Clayton felt his arm grasped, and Hicks stood swaying before him.

"Whyn't ye dance?" he repeated. " Can't ye dance? Mebbe ye air too good-like Sherd. Well, Easter kin, Hyar, Mart, come 'n' dance with the gal. She air the best dancer in these parts."

Clayton had his hand upon Easter as though to forbid her. The mountaineer saw the movement, and his face flamed; but before he could speak, the girl pressed Clayton's arm, and, with an appealing glance, rose to her feet.

That's right," said her father, approvingly, but with a look of drunken malignancy toward Clayton. "Now," he called out, in a loud voice, "I want this couple to have the floor, 'n' everybody to look on 'n' see what is dancin'. Start the fiddles, boys."

It was dancing. The young mountaineer was a slender, active fellow, not without grace, and Easter seemed hardly to touch the floor. They began very slowly at first, till Easter, glancing aside at Clayton and seeing his face deepen with interest, and urged by the remonstrance of het father, the remarks of the onlookers, and the increasing abandon of the music, gave herself up to the dance. The young mountaineer was no mean partner. Forward and back they glided, their swift feet beating every note of the music; Faster receding before her partner, and now advancing toward him, now whirling away with a disdainful toss of her head and arms, and now giving him her hand and whirling till her white skirts floated from the floor. At last, with head bent coquettishly toward her partner, she danced around him, and when it seemed that she would be caught by his outstretched hands she slipped from his clasp, and, with burning cheeks, flashing eyes, and bridal wreath showering its pink-flecked petals about her, flew to Clayton's side.

Mebbe ye don't like that," cried Hicks, turning to Raines, who had been gravely watching the scene.

Raines said nothing in reply, but only looked the drunken man in the face.

"You two," he continued, indicating Clayton with an angry shake of his head, " air a-tryin' to spile ever'body's fun. Both of ye air too high-heeled fer us folks. Y'u hev got mighty good now that ye air a preacher," he added, with a drunken sneer, irritated beyond endurance by Raines's silence and his steady look. "I want ye to know Bill Hicks air a-runnin' things here, 'n' I don't want no meddlin'. I'll drink right here in front o' ye "-holding a bottle defiantly above his head-" 'n' I mean to dance, too, I warn ye now," he added, staggering toward the door, "I don't want no med-dlin'."

Easter had buried her face in her hands. Her mother stood near her husband, helplessly trying to get him away, and fearing to arouse him more. Raines was the most composed man in the room, and a few moments later, when dancing was resumed, Clayton heard his voice at his ear:

"You'd better go upstairs 'n' wait till it's time to go," he said. " He hev got roused ag'in ye, and ag'in me too. I'll keep out o' his way so as not to aggravate him, but I'll stay hyar fer fear something will happen. Mebbe he'll sober up a little, but I'm afeard he'll drink more'n ever."

A moment later, unseen by the rest, the two mounted the stairway to the little room where Easter's girlhood had been passed. To Clayton the peace of the primitive little chamber was an infinite relief. A dim light showed a rude bed in one corner and a pine table close by, whereon lay a few books and a pen and an ink-bottle. Above, the roof rose to a sharp angle, and the low, unplastered walls were covered with pietures cut from the books he had given her. A single window opened into the night over the valley and to the mountains beyond. Two small cane-bottom chairs were near this, and in these they sat down. In the east dark clouds were moving swiftly across the face of the moon, checking its light anJ giving the dim valley startling depth and blackness. Rain-drops struck the roof at intervals, a shower of apple-blossoms rustled against the window and drifted on, and below the muffled sound of music and shuffling feet was now and then pierced by the shrill calls of the prompter. There was something ominous in the persistent tread of feet and the steady flight of the gloomy clouds, and quivering with vague fears, Easter sank down from her chair to Clayton's feet, and burst into tears, as he put his arms tenderly about her.

Has he ever treated you badly?

" No, no," she answered; "it's only the whiskey."

It was not alone of her father's behavior that she was thinking. Memories were busy within her, and a thousand threads of feeling were tightening her love of home, the only home she had ever known. Now she was leaving it for a strange world of which she knew nothing, and the thought pierced her like a physical pain.

"Are we ever coming back ag'in?" she asked, with sudden fear.

Yes, dear," answered Clayton, divining her thoughts; "whenever you wish."

After that she grew calmer, and remained quiet so long that she seemed to have fallen asleep like a tired child relieved of its fears. Leaning forward, he looked into the darkness. It was after midnight, surely. The clouds had become lighter, more luminous, and gradually the moon broke through them, lifting the pall from the valley, playing about the edge of the forest, and quivering at last on the window. As he bent back to look at the sleeping girl, the moonlight fell softly upon her face, revealing its purity of color, and touching the loosened folds of her hair, and shining through a tear-drop which had escaped from her closed lashes. How lovely the face was! How pure! How child-like with all its hidden strength! How absolute her confidence in him! How great her love! It was of her love that he thought, not of his own; but with a new realization of her dependence upon him for happiness, his clasp tightened about her almost unconsciously. She stirred slightly, and, bending his head lower, Clayton whispered in her ear:

Have you been asleep, dear?

She lifted her face and looked tenderly into his eyes, shaking her head slowly, and then, as he bent over again, she clasped her arms about his neck and strained his face to hers.

Not until the opening of the door at the stair-way stirred them did they notice that the music and dancing below had ceased. The door was instantly closed again after a slight sound of scuffling, and in the moment of stillness that followed, they heard Raines say calmly:

"No; you can't go up thar."

A brutal oath answered him, and Easter started to her feet when she heard her father's voice, terrible with passion; but Clayton held her back, and hurried down the stairway.

"Ef ye don't come away from that door," he could hear Hicks saying, " 'n' stop this meddlin', I'll kill you 'stid o' the furriner."

As Clayton thrust the door open, Raines was standing a few feet from the stairway. The drunken man was struggling in the grasp of several mountaineers, who were coaxing and dragging him across the room. About them were several other men scarcely able to stand, and behind these a crowd of shrinking women.

Git back! git back! " said Raines, in low, hurried tones.

But Hicks had caught sight of Clayton. For a moment he stood still, glaring at him. Then, with a furious effort, he wrenched himself from the men who held him, and thrust his hand into his pocket, backing against the wall. The crowd fell away from him as a weapon was drawn and levelled with unsteady hand at Clayton. Raines sprang forward; Clayton felt his arm clutched, and a figure darted past him. The flash came, and when Raines wrenched the weapon from the mountaineer's grasp the latter was standing rigid, with horror-stricken eyes fixed upon the smoke, in which Easter's white face showed like an apparition. As the smoke drifted aside, the girl was seen with both hands at her breast. Then, while a silent terror held every one, she turned, and, with outstretched hands, tottered toward Clayton; and as he caught her in his arms, a low moan broke from her lips.

Some one hurried away for a physician, but the death-watch was over before he came.

For a long time the wounded girl lay apparently unconscious, her face white and quiet. Only when a wood-thrush called from the woods close by were her lids half raised, and as Clayton pushed the shutter open above her and lifted her gently, she opened her eyes with a grateful look and turned her face eagerly to the cool air.

The dawn was breaking. The east was already aflame with bars of rosy light, gradually widening. Above them a single star was poised, and in the valley below great white mists were stirring from sleep. For a moment she seemed to be listlessly watching the white, shapeless things, trembling as with life, and creeping silently into wood and up glen; and then her lashes drooped wearily together.

The door opened as Clayton let her sink upon the bed, breathing as if asleep, and he turned, expecting the physician. Raines, too, rose eagerly, stopped suddenly, and shrank back with a shudder of repulsion as the figure of the wretched father crept, half crouching, within.

Sherd!

The girl's tone was full of gentle reproach, and so soft that it reached only Clayton's ears.

Sherd!

This time his name was uttered with an appeal ever so gentle.

Pore dad! Pore dad! " she whispered. Her clasp tightened suddenly on Clayton's hand, and her eyes were held to his, even while the light in them was going out.

A week later two men left the cabin at dusk.

Half-way down the slope they came to one of the unspeakably mournful little burying-grounds wherein the mountain people rest after their narrow lives. It was unhedged, uncared for, and a few crumbling boards for headstones told the living generation where the dead were at rest. For a moment they paused to look at a spot under a great beech where the earth had been lately disturbed.

"It air shorely hard to see," said one in a low, slow voice, "why she was taken, 'n1 him left; why she should hev to give her life fer the life he took. But He knows, He knows," the mountaineer continued, with unfaltering trust; and then, after a moment's struggle to reconcile fact with faith: "The Lord took whut He keered fer most, 'n' she was ready, 'n' he wasn t.

The other made no reply, and they kept on in silence. Upon a spur of the mountain beneath which the little mining-town had sunk to quiet for the night they parted with a hand-clasp. Not till then was the silence broken.

"Thar seems to be a penalty fer lovin' too ''much down hyar," said one; " 'n' I reckon," he added, slowly, "that both of us hev got hit to pay."

Turning, the speaker retraced his steps. The other kept on toward the lights below.

THE END

The Codes Of Hammurabi And Moses
W. W. Davies

QTY

The discovery of the Hammurabi Code is one of the greatest achievements of archaeology, and is of paramount interest, not only to the student of the Bible, but also to all those interested in ancient history...

Religion   ISBN: *1-59462-338-4*

Pages:132
MSRP $12.95

The Theory of Moral Sentiments
Adam Smith

QTY

This work from 1749. contains original theories of conscience amd moral judgment and it is the foundation for systemof morals.

Philosophy   ISBN: *1-59462-777-0*

Pages:536
MSRP $19.95

Jessica's First Prayer
Hesba Stretton

QTY

In a screened and secluded corner of one of the many railway-bridges which span the streets of London there could be seen a few years ago, from five o'clock every morning until half past eight, a tidily set-out coffee-stall, consisting of a trestle and board, upon which stood two large tin cans, with a small fire of charcoal burning under each so as to keep the coffee boiling during the early hours of the morning when the work-people were thronging into the city on their way to their daily toil...

Pages:84

Childrens   ISBN: *1-59462-373-2*

MSRP $9.95

My Life and Work
Henry Ford

QTY

Henry Ford revolutionized the world with his implementation of mass production for the Model T automobile. Gain valuable business insight into his life and work with his own auto-biography... "We have only started on our development of our country we have not as yet, with all our talk of wonderful progress, done more than scratch the surface. The progress has been wonderful enough but..."

Pages:300

Biographies/   ISBN: *1-59462-198-5*

MSRP $21.95

The Art of Cross-Examination
Francis Wellman

QTY

I presume it is the experience of every author, after his first book is published upon an important subject, to be almost overwhelmed with a wealth of ideas and illustrations which could readily have been included in his book, and which to his own mind, at least, seem to make a second edition inevitable. Such certainly was the case with me; and when the first edition had reached its sixth impression in five months, I rejoiced to learn that it seemed to my publishers that the book had met with a sufficiently favorable reception to justify a second and considerably enlarged edition. ..

Pages:412

Reference   **ISBN: *1-59462-647-2***   *MSRP $19.95*

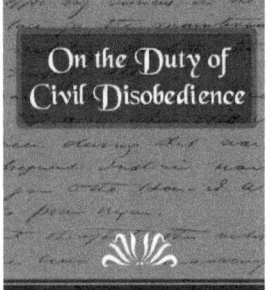

On the Duty of Civil Disobedience
Henry David Thoreau

QTY

Thoreau wrote his famous essay, On the Duty of Civil Disobedience, as a protest against an unjust but popular war and the immoral but popular institution of slave-owning. He did more than write—he declined to pay his taxes, and was hauled off to gaol in consequence. Who can say how much this refusal of his hastened the end of the war and of slavery ?

Law   **ISBN: *1-59462-747-9***   **Pages:48**

MSRP $7.45

Dream Psychology Psychoanalysis for Beginners
Sigmund Freud

QTY

Sigmund Freud, born Sigismund Schlomo Freud (May 6, 1856 - September 23, 1939), was a Jewish-Austrian neurologist and psychiatrist who co-founded the psychoanalytic school of psychology. Freud is best known for his theories of the unconscious mind, especially involving the mechanism of repression; his redefinition of sexual desire as mobile and directed towards a wide variety of objects; and his therapeutic techniques, especially his understanding of transference in the therapeutic relationship and the presumed value of dreams as sources of insight into unconscious desires.

Pages:196

Psychology   **ISBN: *1-59462-905-6***   *MSRP $15.45*

The Miracle of Right Thought
Orison Swett Marden

QTY

Believe with all of your heart that you will do what you were made to do. When the mind has once formed the habit of holding cheerful, happy, prosperous pictures, it will not be easy to form the opposite habit. It does not matter how improbable or how far away this realization may see, or how dark the prospects may be, if we visualize them as best we can, as vividly as possible, hold tenaciously to them and vigorously struggle to attain them, they will gradually become actualized, realized in the life. But a desire, a longing without endeavor, a yearning abandoned or held indifferently will vanish without realization.

Pages:360

Self Help   **ISBN: *1-59462-644-8***   *MSRP $25.45*

The Rosicrucian Cosmo-Conception Mystic Christianity *by Max Heindel*   ISBN: *1-59462-188-8*   **$38.95**
The Rosicrucian Cosmo-conception is not dogmatic, neither does it appeal to any other authority than the reason of the student. It is: not controversial, but is: sent forth in the, hope that it may help to clear..   *New Age/Religion Pages 646*

Abandonment To Divine Providence *by Jean-Pierre de Caussade*   ISBN: *1-59462-228-0*   **$25.95**
"The Rev. Jean Pierre de Caussade was one of the most remarkable spiritual writers of the Society of Jesus in France in the 18th Century. His death took place at Toulouse in 1751. His works have gone through many editions and have been republished...   *Inspirational/Religion Pages 400*

Mental Chemistry *by Charles Haanel*   ISBN: *1-59462-192-6*   **$23.95**
Mental Chemistry allows the change of material conditions by combining and appropriately utilizing the power of the mind. Much like applied chemistry creates something new and unique out of careful combinations of chemicals the mastery of mental chemistry...   *New Age Pages 354*

The Letters of Robert Browning and Elizabeth Barret Barrett 1845-1846 vol II   ISBN: *1-59462-193-4*   **$35.95**
by Robert Browning and Elizabeth Barrett   *Biographies Pages 596*

Gleanings In Genesis (volume I) *by Arthur W. Pink*   ISBN: *1-59462-130-6*   **$27.45**
Appropriately has Genesis been termed "the seed plot of the Bible" for in it we have, in germ form, almost all of the great doctrines which are afterwards fully developed in the books of Scripture which follow...   *Religion/Inspirational Pages 420*

The Master Key *by L. W. de Laurence*   ISBN: *1-59462-001-6*   **$30.95**
In no branch of human knowledge has there been a more lively increase of the spirit of research during the past few years than in the study of Psychology, Concentration and Mental Discipline. The requests for authentic lessons in Thought Control, Mental Discipline and...   *New Age/Business Pages 422*

The Lesser Key Of Solomon Goetia *by L. W. de Laurence*   ISBN: *1-59462-092-X*   **$9.95**
This translation of the first book of the "Lemegton" which is now for the first time made accessible to students of Talismanic Magic was done, after careful collation and edition, from numerous Ancient Manuscripts in Hebrew, Latin, and French...   *New Age/Occult Pages 92*

Rubaiyat Of Omar Khayyam *by Edward Fitzgerald*   ISBN:*1-59462-332-5*   **$13.95**
Edward Fitzgerald, whom the world has already learned, in spite of his own efforts to remain within the shadow of anonymity, to look upon as one of the rarest poets of the century, was born at Bredfield, in Suffolk, on the 31st of March, 1809. He was the third son of John Purcell...   *Music Pages 172*

Ancient Law *by Henry Maine*   ISBN: *1-59462-128-4*   **$29.95**
The chief object of the following pages is to indicate some of the earliest ideas of mankind, as they are reflected in Ancient Law, and to point out the relation of those ideas to modern thought.   *Religiom/History Pages 452*

Far-Away Stories *by William J. Locke*   ISBN: *1-59462-129-2*   **$19.45**
"Good wine needs no bush, but a collection of mixed vintages does. And this book is just such a collection. Some of the stories I do not want to remain buried for ever in the museum files of dead magazine-numbers an author's not unpardonable vanity..."   *Fiction Pages 272*

Life of David Crockett *by David Crockett*   ISBN: *1-59462-250-7*   **$27.45**
"Colonel David Crockett was one of the most remarkable men of the times in which he lived. Born in humble life, but gifted with a strong will, an indomitable courage, and unremitting perseverance...   *Biographies/New Age Pages 424*

Lip-Reading *by Edward Nitchie*   ISBN: *1-59462-206-X*   **$25.95**
Edward B. Nitchie, founder of the New York School for the Hard of Hearing, now the Nitchie School of Lip-Reading, Inc, wrote "LIP-READING Principles and Practice". The development and perfecting of this meritorious work on lip-reading was an undertaking...   *How-to Pages 400*

A Handbook of Suggestive Therapeutics, Applied Hypnotism, Psychic Science   ISBN: *1-59462-214-0*   **$24.95**
by Henry Munro   *Health/New Age/Health/Self-help Pages 376*

A Doll's House: and Two Other Plays *by Henrik Ibsen*   ISBN: *1-59462-112-8*   **$19.95**
Henrik Ibsen created this classic when in revolutionary 1848 Rome. Introducing some striking concepts in playwriting for the realist genre, this play has been studied the world over.   *Fiction/Classics/Plays 308*

The Light of Asia *by sir Edwin Arnold*   ISBN: *1-59462-204-3*   **$13.95**
In this poetic masterpiece, Edwin Arnold describes the life and teachings of Buddha. The man who was to become known as Buddha to the world was born as Prince Gautama of India but he rejected the worldly riches and abandoned the reigns of power when... Religion/History/Biographies Pages 170

The Complete Works of Guy de Maupassant *by Guy de Maupassant*   ISBN: *1-59462-157-8*   **$16.95**
"For days and days, nights and nights, I had dreamed of that first kiss which was to consecrate our engagement, and I knew not on what spot I should put my lips..."   *Fiction/Classics Pages 240*

The Art of Cross-Examination *by Francis L. Wellman*   ISBN: *1-59462-309-0*   **$26.95**
Written by a renowned trial lawyer, Wellman imparts his experience and uses case studies to explain how to use psychology to extract desired information through questioning.   *How-to/Science/Reference Pages 408*

Answered or Unanswered? *by Louisa Vaughan*   ISBN: *1-59462-248-5*   **$10.95**
Miracles of Faith in China   *Religion Pages 112*

The Edinburgh Lectures on Mental Science (1909) *by Thomas*   ISBN: *1-59462-008-3*   **$11.95**
This book contains the substance of a course of lectures recently given by the writer in the Queen Street Hail, Edinburgh. Its purpose is to indicate the Natural Principles governing the relation between Mental Action and Material Conditions...   *New Age/Psychology Pages 148*

Ayesha *by H. Rider Haggard*   ISBN: *1-59462-301-5*   **$24.95**
Verily and indeed it is the unexpected that happens! Probably if there was one person upon the earth from whom the Editor of this, and of a certain previous history, did not expect to hear again...   *Classics Pages 380*

Ayala's Angel *by Anthony Trollope*   ISBN: *1-59462-352-X*   **$29.95**
The two girls were both pretty, but Lucy who was twenty-one who supposed to be simple and comparatively unattractive, whereas Ayala was credited, as her Bombwhat romantic name might show, with poetic charm and a taste for romance. Ayala when her father died was nineteen...   *Fiction Pages 484*

The American Commonwealth *by James Bryce*   ISBN: *1-59462-286-8*   **$34.45**
An interpretation of American democratic political theory. It examines political mechanics and society from the perspective of Scotsman James Bryce   *Politics Pages 572*

Stories of the Pilgrims *by Margaret P. Pumphrey*   ISBN: *1-59462-116-0*   **$17.95**
This book explores pilgrims religious oppression in England as well as their escape to Holland and eventual crossing to America on the Mayflower, and their early days in New England...   *History Pages 268*

QTY

The Fasting Cure *by Sinclair Upton* ISBN: *1-59462-222-1* **$13.95**
In the Cosmopolitan Magazine for May, 1910, and in the Contemporary Review (London) for April, 1910, I published an article dealing with my experiences in fasting. I have written a great many magazine articles, but never one which attracted so much attention... New Age/Self Help/Health Pages 164

Hebrew Astrology *by Sepharial* ISBN: *1-59462-308-2* **$13.45**
In these days of advanced thinking it is a matter of common observation that we have left many of the old landmarks behind and that we are now pressing forward to greater heights and to a wider horizon than that which represented the mind-content of our progenitors... Astrology Pages 144

Thought Vibration or The Law of Attraction in the Thought World ISBN: *1-59462-127-6* **$12.95**
by William Walker Atkinson Psychology/Religion Pages 144

Optimism *by Helen Keller* ISBN: *1-59462-108-X* **$15.95**
Helen Keller was blind, deaf, and mute since 19 months old, yet famously learned how to overcome these handicaps, communicate with the world, and spread her lectures promoting optimism. An inspiring read for everyone... Biographies/Inspirational Pages 84

Sara Crewe *by Frances Burnett* ISBN: *1-59462-360-0* **$9.45**
In the first place, Miss Minchin lived in London. Her home was a large, dull, tall one, in a large, dull square, where all the houses were alike, and all the sparrows were alike, and where all the door-knockers made the same heavy sound... Childrens/Classic Pages 88

The Autobiography of Benjamin Franklin *by Benjamin Franklin* ISBN: *1-59462-135-7* **$24.95**
The Autobiography of Benjamin Franklin has probably been more extensively read than any other American historical work, and no other book of its kind has had such ups and downs of fortune. Franklin lived for many years in England, where he was agent... Biographies/History Pages 332

Name	
Email	
Telephone	
Address	
City, State ZIP	

☐ **Credit Card**   ☐ **Check / Money Order**

Credit Card Number	
Expiration Date	
Signature	

Please Mail to: Book Jungle
PO Box 2226
Champaign, IL 61825
or Fax to: 630-214-0564

ORDERING INFORMATION

web: *www.bookjungle.com*
email: *sales@bookjungle.com*
fax: *630-214-0564*
mail: *Book Jungle PO Box 2226 Champaign, IL 61825*
or PayPal *to sales@bookjungle.com*

Please contact us for bulk discounts

DIRECT-ORDER TERMS

**20% Discount if You Order
Two or More Books**
Free Domestic Shipping!
Accepted: Master Card, Visa,
Discover, American Express